Layovers Collection
Vol. 1

A TASTE
of
Temptation

SASKIA LAINE

A Ganache Media Book

Vancouver

If you are reading this book as a PDF, you have obtained a pirated, unauthorized edition, and are contributing to the marginalization of authors' incomes. We hope you enjoy your latte, which cost more than an authorized edition of this book, and took a fraction of the time to prepare.

If you bought this book, thank you, and we unironically hope you're enjoying it with the best latte you ever tasted. You probably tipped your barista too, because you're awesome.

This book is a work of fiction. Names, characters, places, and incidents either are the product of the author's imagination, or are used fictitiously. Any resemblance to actual persons, living or dead, events, or locales is entirely coincidental.

2020 Ganache Media print edition

ISBN 978-1-988293-13-4

Cover design by Katrina Archer
www.ganachemedia.com
saskialaine.com

CONTENTS

Sins of OMISSION

CHAPTER ONE

THE plane yawed and dropped precipitously, as though whatever current of air supporting the wings had momentarily disappeared. A child behind me shrieked. My stomach lurched to my throat and I said a silent prayer to the holy trinity of aerodynamics, air traffic control, and aircraft maintenance.

Lightning flashed outside the window and I swallowed bile. I bent forward for my purse, but it squatted on the floor out of reach, and there was no way I was unbuckling my seatbelt now. I stretched my foot out to try to nudge the bag into range, but the extra business-class legroom taunted me.

"Come *on* ..."

I really needed those ginger pills.

The plane dove again and I dry heaved.

As the pilot fought the weather trying to bring us safely into the island, I squeezed my eyes shut and white-knuckled my armrests. *Breathe through your nose, Lash. Just breathe through your nose.*

Easier said than done when your plane was acting like a rollercoaster.

Thunder roared outside, way too close. The plane shuddered. My eyes sprang open.

A barf bag hovered in the air in front of me. I frowned in puzzlement, then saw the hand holding it. I snatched the bag and visually followed the hand along a narrow wrist, to an arm encased in a grey linen suit, which was connected to my row mate across the aisle. I'd noticed him while boarding, trim and tall and handsome enough to earn a second glance, but he'd pointedly avoided conversation as we'd settled in for the flight.

"Thank you. I hate small planes."

He shrugged, and turned back to his laptop. "I could do without a mess."

I almost snarked back about what I could do without as well, but the plane plunged and a desperate urge swept over me to make sure I got that bag open, and kept my mouth shut until I did. As I held the bag close to my face, I snuck a glance to my right. Linen Suit blithely typed away at a document. Who could possibly work under conditions like this?

Irritating row mates, apparently.

We dipped below the cloud layer and just like that, the plane stabilized. As we cleared the storm cell, sun glinted off the waves of the Mediterranean below us, and I spotted Corsica off to the left. The pilot banked to take us into Figari-Sud airport, and my stomach contracted worryingly once before the prospect of solid ground began to settle it. Before I knew it, we were rumbling down the runway.

With the seatbelt sign turned off, I stood and opened the overhead bin. My laptop bag, dislodged by the turbulence, tumbled out. I caught it awkwardly before it slammed into the aisle, but jostled Linen Suit.

"I'm so sorry."

He shot me an annoyed look, then stood, stooping to fit his long frame beneath the overhead compartment. He pushed past me to the forward door of the plane.

"Not at all. Thank you for not letting your laptop smash my head in," I muttered under my breath. *Some people.*

I made my way down the stairs and across the tarmac. After a minimal wait for my checked bag, I exited the tiny terminal, glad to leave the scent of jet fuel behind me, and found the Conlan Corsica Resort's shuttle. +10 points for no waiting. Linen Suit was already seated kitty-corner from the driver.

"I guess we're going to the same place," I said brightly.

He gave me a flat stare from beneath heavy dark brows as I slipped past him to the back of the van, but he didn't say a word.

I crossed my eyes at the back of his head. *Be that way.*

Since I could reach them now, I dug a ginger pill out of my purse for the trip to Palombaggia, a little southeast of the town of Porto-Vecchio. My previous experiences with aggressive French driving had me forewarned. I'm just not a very good passenger.

We pulled into the resort thirty minutes later and I took a deep lungful of fresh, seaside air. The driveway still glistened from the squall's rain shower. A riot of purple bougainvillea cascaded over the stone walls. +10 points for landscaping. I liked this place already, but reminded myself I wasn't here to like it.

Linen Suit marched off to reception—he traveled light—while I waited for the driver to get my bag out of the trunk. I trundled into the main lobby and gave it a quick scan while I waited for my erstwhile traveling companion to check in. Tile floors and rustic logs beams across the ceiling blended with pale walls and warm wooden millwork to create a pleasing balance between traditional and modern.

"*Oui monsieur. Votre villa préférée est prête.*" The woman at the front desk handed Linen Suit a keycard. "*Attendez un moment, je crois que vous avez reçu un colis.*" She disappeared into a room behind the desk, while Linen Suit stepped aside to wait. +10 points for personalized service with attention to detail.

Another woman stepped behind the desk and smiled at me. "*Bon après-midi. Puis-je vous aider?* Can I help you?"

"I'm Lashka Wright. I have a reservation?" It behooved me to keep my fluent French on the down-low for the moment.

"*Bien sûr*, Ms. Wright. If I could see your passport and a credit card, please?"

I handed over the documents and she checked me in efficiently. A good sign, and another 10 points on my little evaluation scale.

She gave me my keycard and a map of the resort. "Your suite is here. Just follow the path past the elevator and out through the courtyard garden."

"Thank you. Do you know if there is a nice hike easily accessible from the resort?" I liked to stretch my legs after a day of traveling.

"There is always the beach, madame."

"I was hoping for something with a little elevation."

The desk clerk hesitated. -10 points for lack of local knowledge.

"I can show you."

Linen Suit talks! I suppressed a double take.

The other clerk bustled out from the back room and placed a package on the counter.

Linen Suit tucked it under his arm. "Follow me."

He walked off and I scrambled to grab map, key, and bags before I lost him. Once past the elevators, he exited the main building, but instead of going through the garden, he turned onto a walkway parallel to the east wing of rooms. The compound was a maze of stacked buildings on multiple levels, with tumbled-stone walls and stairs, surrounding a central courtyard containing the garden and an infinity pool, which in turn led to the main bar and patio areas, and hotel restaurant. Private nooks and crannies abounded in the twisting pathways, which meant if I lost him, I'd be in trouble.

"I—"

He kept walking.

"It's just—"

He stopped. Gave me an impatient glance from beneath his artfully tousled black bangs.

"Is it very far? I was hoping to drop off my bags before exploring too much." The multilevel layout made dragging my bag around that much harder, since Linen Suit had taken off so quickly I hadn't had a chance to snag a bellhop.

He muttered an imprecation, though all I caught was "…time for this." Then he marched back past me. "See that?" He pointed at one of the private villas at the edge of the compound. "Meet me in front of it in fifteen minutes."

"If it's too much trouble, I can always get the front desk to show me." But he'd already stalked off, messenger bag banging against his hip, and parcel wedged under his arm.

I swung my roller bag around and followed him more slowly, the map from reception telling me my room lay in one of the outer buildings near his. It had a ground-level entrance, and when I got through the door I found an immaculate suite with an expansive seating area, kitchenette, and private bedroom, all decorated with the ubiquitous tile floors and a clean white-plus-wood-accents palette.

My room contained a modern four-post bed complete with sheer linen tieback curtains. A window wall opened out to the patio at the back, shaded by a rustic wood pergola. The view from there looked out over the low hills to the beach, the turquoise water of the Mediterranean sparkling in the sun. +50 points for cleanliness. +100 for atmosphere.

I dropped my laptop bag on the couch and dragged my

suitcase into the bedroom, heaving it up onto the bag stand I found already deployed (+5 points). I kicked off my wedges, changed into light exercise gear, and slipped on my cross trainers. I grabbed a glass of water and slathered on some sunscreen, even though the bronze skin I'd inherited from my mother didn't burn that easily. This far south it didn't hurt to be careful. Then I tucked my unruly dark hair into a pony tail and headed out again to meet Mr. Grumpy. The new name fit him better.

He was waiting for me outside the villa, which I knew was a swankier version of my suite, with more rooms and an oversized private patio. Some of the villas had outdoor spas. Traveling light and living large, Mr. Grumpy was.

He didn't even greet me as I arrived, just spun on his heel and took off at a brisk walk. *Nice to see you again too.* He was still wearing his linen pants, but had shed the suit jacket. With his chiseled features and the five o'clock shadow stubbling his jaw, I wouldn't have minded more time to look at him, if he could only stop scowling and act like a human being. But that didn't seem to be in the cards.

Instead of going back to the initial walkway we'd been on, he headed past his villa, where the path followed the stone perimeter fence. We went through a wrought-iron gate, and found ourselves in a maintenance area of the resort, with a parking lot and storage sheds for the landscapers. He led me past these to a trail leading up an embankment. He started up it.

"Thanks! I think I can take it from here."

"You'll just get lost. I'll come with."

Uuuh. No? I just wanted a little quiet time to myself and a leg stretch? "My mother always said not to follow strange men." *Talking* to this strange man didn't look like it would be an issue.

"My name's Kellan." He set off again, as if that should make us bosom buddies.

"I'm Lashka!" I shouted after him. "Nice to meet you," I muttered.

He crested the embankment. "Are you coming or not?"

"Are you an ax murderer?"

He rolled his eyes, disappeared down the hill on the other side.

I blinked for half a breath at the empty skyline where he'd just been, then sighed and trotted up the hill after him. Ax murderers weren't known for their side-eye.

With his long legs, he traveled at a good clip, so I had to trot to catch up. The trail zigzagged in a generally north-northwesterly direction along the hillside above Palombaggia, through low scrub. After the recent rainfall, the vegetation smelled of savory and spice, the air crisp and clean, with a faint lingering ozony tang leftover from the storm. I wondered if this area was part of the famous Corsican maquis.

At first it felt weird following this guy along the trail in utter silence, but he set a pace that suited me, and the lack of conversation did give me the quiet I'd been craving after that brutal flight in.

And he'd been right: spurs and junctions abounded, I presumed following local herding routes. Or maybe they were there just to confuse the tourists. I wouldn't have gotten lost, exactly, because you could see the whole valley and beaches laid out to the south below us, and we never lost sight of the resort. But I would have made plenty of false starts and wasted time trying to figure out a route that didn't double back on itself. Which would have been fine for the purpose of stretching my legs, but having a private tour guide saved me some trouble.

Plus I had a great view of his ass, a pleasingly proportioned bonus. He'd started to perspire, his shirt clinging to his back between his shoulder blades. His long dark hair fluttered in the ocean breeze, and I had to admit, he pulled off casually disheveled beach chic quite well from this vantage point, though I didn't think I could credit a points bonus to the hotel for his presence. His personality might cancel out his physique, anyway.

We climbed a set of switchbacks, setting my heart rate skyrocketing, but at the top found ourselves on a ridge with an expansive view of the coastline. Kellan stopped to let me catch my breath, not looking at all winded himself, which might be explained by his wiry runner's physique.

White sand beaches contoured small bays separated by rocky promontories and hills covered with dark green scrub. The breeze blew in strongly from the ocean, and the squall line still loomed to the north of us. The larger town of Porto-Vecchio lay nestled along the bay to the north and west of us, while Palombaggia and Tamaricciu beaches sparkled to the south.

Kellan pointed to a trail leading almost due east from us down the hillside. "This goes down to that small bay there, which is worth a look because most of the tourists can't find it."

"It speaks!"

Very funny, his look said. Now that he'd spoken more than half a dozen words in a row to me, I discerned an Irish lilt to his voice.

"You must come here a lot if you can find your way around like this."

"Yes."

Open-ended questions, Lashka. Open. Ended. Or it might be easier to just give up on conversation entirely.

"Is that enough of a walk for you?"

I decided that it was. I'd gotten enough fresh air and exercise to flush the last vestiges of small-plane syndrome from my mood. "Yes. Thank you. I think I'll be able to find this again too."

He nodded and without another word—surprise, surprise—set off back down the hill.

When we got back to the resort, he didn't even wait to close the gate before marching up the path to his villa. I jogged to catch him before he disappeared inside.

"You don't like to talk much, do you?"

"Not when I don't have anything to say."

"Well, anyway, thank you. I appreciate you schlepping me

around the Corsican countryside. I know you didn't have to."

"I needed to clear my head too." He gave me a small smile and I nearly fainted from shock. "And you're welcome." Then he disappeared into his villa without so much as a wave.

"Bye to you too." I wandered back to my suite in search of room service and a good glass of French wine.

CHAPTER TWO

I only had three days to complete my evaluation, so I had to plan my time carefully and hit the ground running. I wouldn't ask for a meeting with the manager until my last day, because this exercise worked best if the properties didn't see me coming.

The real estate portfolio management firm I worked for had sent me to determine if the Conlan Corsica was their kind of investment. Chris Conlan was divesting himself of a few key resorts in the Conlan chain in order to focus on urban hotels, and this one had twigged Pritchard, Hanson & Vale's interest. They had done all the due diligence on the financials, but my job was to assess the intangibles.

I had a quantitative scale for things like service, atmosphere, and level of upkeep, but PHV had hired me because I had a good gut instinct for what made a holiday property attractive in the long run, which didn't just mean evaluating the resort but its environs as well—another reason for my little hike yesterday: I liked putting my boots to the ground and immersing myself in the local flavor.

To be honest, I had the Best Job Ever^{TM}—paid travel at some of the finest hotels in sought-after locations around the world—and never ceased to thank my lucky stars that PHV liked to think outside the box. The occasional bout of airsickness was worth the hassle.

On my first day I took breakfast at the resort restaurant —I'd eat at least one meal a day there to see how they did at different times of the day and if the service was consistent— then checked out the pool and other facilities. Around lunchtime I spent a couple of hours exploring Porto-Vecchio itself, admiring the shiny luxury yachts in its harbor before walking up the hill and intentionally losing myself in the restaurant-lined cobbled streets of the old town. I snacked on an excellent seafood salad, then I returned to do that longer hike to the bay Kellan had pointed out.

Which, true to his word, I had almost completely to myself. Unlike the other local beaches, this one was in a nature preserve and had been left wild. It didn't boast the typical beach bars present at most other spots, but what it lacked in amenities, it made up for in secluded charm. The fifteen-minute walk in from the only road nearby discouraged casual visitors. A small pond separated the beach from the inland scrub, and the clear turquoise waters of the Med lapped against pristine white sand. A couple of backpackers had set up their tent at the northern tip of the beach.

I splashed around in the sea for a bit, enjoying the refreshing embrace of salt water against my skin after my walk. It would hopefully keep me cool for the journey back.

Throughout the day, the Conlan Corsica had been racking up points in my quantitative scale. The place was impeccably maintained and the staff attentive, without the snootiness that French hotels sometimes suffered from. The only fly in the ointment came when I returned from my hike just before sunset to find the air conditioning in my room on the fritz. -250 points.

"I'm so sorry, Ms. Wright," the front desk said when I called. "We'll send someone over right away to look into it. Would you like to wait at the bar? It will be with our compliments for the inconvenience. Dinner is on us as well."

Free drinks? Why not. +100.

I rinsed off the hiking dust and slipped into a light cotton blouse and flowy, asymmetrical skirt, switching out my cross trainers for my wedges. Then I wandered down to the bar, where a number of people were having end-of-day sundowners as the sun disappeared behind the mountains. The murmur of conversation in several European languages drifted out over the pool. The patio was crowded, so I took a seat at the counter that bordered it, and ordered a very dry vodka martini with a lemon twist.

I was sipping my drink in quiet contemplation, going over the day's discoveries in my head, writing down some items to review in my notebook, when a strong odor of rum wafted over me.

"Hey there, gorgeous." *Oh no.* A man entirely too enamored with his own muscles—based on the too-tight T-shirt stretched across his pecs—pulled out the stool next to mine. He had the look of someone who spent excessive amounts of time oiling himself at the beach, his hair spiky and over-gelled. "Can I buy you a drink?"

I held up my three-quarters-full martini glass. "I'm fine, thanks."

He leaned in closer to me and my eyes watered from the vapors. "Well, then, let's just get to know each other better."

Let's not, asshole. "I'm kind of busy." I picked up my pen again.

He flicked a finger at my pen, marring my notes. "Come on, baby. Why work when you can talk to Nick?" Nick from New Jersey, from the sound of it. He covered my hand with his and squeezed. "Working too hard ages you early, and you don't want those laugh lines getting bigger do you?"

Negging, too. Great. "Let go of my hand. Now." A German couple on the patio glanced up at my tone.

Nick threw up his hands. "Okay, okay! No need for drama." He took a swig of his rum and Coke and stared out at the ocean while I pointedly jotted down nonsense in my notebook, ignoring him with prejudice.

He spun suddenly and knocked over my martini glass, spilling vodka all over my carefully annotated pages. "Aw. Lookit that. Now I need to buy you that drink."

"Dude! I said *no*." I sopped up as much liquid as I could and hurriedly swept my notebook into my purse, praying the hotel had fixed my air conditioning already. I hopped off the stool.

Nick blocked my exit, grabbed my arm just above the elbow. "Come on. Don't be that way. I'm just tryin' to be friendly." There was nothing friendly about his hold on my arm. I shot a look over to the bar but the bartender was on the phone with someone, and I didn't see a bouncer. -1000 for not keeping an eye on guests' physical security.

"If you just let me make it up to you, I know we can have some fun."

I tried to shake his hand off but he tightened his grip, moving into my personal space. The reek of alcohol made me cough. My heart took off at the races. I fought the urge to freeze like a frightened rabbit. I raised my voice. "Get your hands *off* me, NOW!" This was a public place, for fuck's sake. *Someone* had to notice what was going on.

Nick jerked my arm. He abandoned his faux nice-guy persona, got right in my face. "Why can't you bitches just relax? I know just how to fix uptight cunts like yours."

Hold it together, Lash. I couldn't let him feel me shaking, even though the fight-or-flight hormones flooding my system had all my nerve ends firing at once. I now knew he wasn't the type who could accept any kind of no for an answer, which ruled out de-escalation. Was he a hitter, too?

Guess I'd find out soon.

I stiff-armed him, pushing him away. He stumbled backward, letting go of me in surprise. "Fuck you, bitch!"

As he recovered, a hand warmed the small of my back and I flinched, startled. Scanning for a new threat, trying not to take my eyes off Nick, I recognized Kellan in my peripheral vision just behind me. He spread his fingers, and I settled like a spooked horse calmed by a reassuring hand on its neck.

"Sorry I'm late," Kellan said. "I got held up on a conference call. Who's your friend?"

Nick glanced from me to Kellan. I could see him trying to figure out if I'd been intending to meet Kellan all along, assessing who had the bigger muscles. Then the douchebag doubled down. "Early bird gets the worm, bro. We were just leaving." He moved to grab me again.

Kellan reacted so quickly, I almost missed what happened. He reached past me, snatched Nick's wrist, then stepped through Nick's motion, bringing Nick's arm up behind his back at a painful angle. Nick yelled and bent over. Kellan leaned over him and spoke into his ear. I just caught his tone, quiet, calm, and deadly, deadly taut with repressed violence. Nick paled—quite a feat beneath his beach-sleazoid tan. Kellan released his arm and Nick stumbled forward. By this time, the bartender had noticed our little drama and I saw a beefy security guard come jogging into the bar.

Kellan kept himself between me and Nick, who was now looking anywhere but at me.

"S-sorry, lady. Sorry. I, uh, gotta go." Nick scuttled away, the security guard following him out.

Kellan brushed his hand against his white shirt as though flicking away an annoying bug.

Now I really started to shake. I grabbed the nearest stool as my knees went wobbly.

"Are you all right?" Kellan put a concerned hand on my shoulder.

"Not yet. But I will be." I swallowed against a sudden urge to cry. "I—Would you excuse me for a moment?" I almost ran to the washroom next to the bar.

I leaned against the tumbled-stone wall and took a series of deep, sobbing breaths, then dashed away the tears—tears of blended rage and fear—with a trembling hand. Why were there so many assholes in the world, and why did they like to target me?

"It's not just you, Lashka," my best friend had once said, but that didn't make me feel any better. I could be the most careful, mind-my-own-business traveler ever, and it didn't seem to matter.

"You're safe, Lash. It's over," I said to myself in the mirror as I splashed water over my face and composed myself. *At least until the next asshole.*

I wouldn't let one idiot ruin this whole trip. One of the best parts of traveling was meeting so many great people. Everyone else here had been lovely—for values of lovely that graded on a bell curve for grumpy. Although Kellan had decidedly just made up for his bad start.

I exited the washroom and found the bartender waiting for me, holding out a tray with a fresh martini. "Compliments of the gentleman on the patio."

Kellan raised a highball glass from his seat at a lounge table. He inclined his head towards the open chair next to him.

I really just wanted the safety of my room right now. But then, it might be smart to wait until I could be sure Nick had disappeared. And I should express my gratitude to my knight in shining cotton.

I picked up the martini glass and made my way over to Kellan.

"Join me?" he asked. I sat down and he reached out to clink my glass. "May the rest of your evening be drama free."

"I'll drink to that." I took a large swig of vodka. It was my turn to not say anything for a while. For the first time, I appreciated Kellan's quietness. He sipped on his gin and tonic, and admired the sunset while I tried not to shiver. It always took me a while to climb down from confrontations like that. The vodka helped.

"Have you eaten? The *calmar* here is topnotch."

I'd worked up an appetite from the hike but before I ate I needed the knot in my belly to unclench a bit more. "Maybe in a little bit?"

"I've no need to crack on. Would you like another?" He nodded at my empty glass.

"Why not?"

Kellan signaled the bartender, who acknowledged and busied himself making us more drinks. "Feeling better?"

"I'll live. Thanks for intervening."

"It looked like you were doing just fine without me. That stiff-arm was a thing of beauty. Fierce."

"Still …"

"Any time." He smiled and it transformed the stern

planes of his face. "I'll take two-to-one odds any day in a fight."

Hot tears welled at the corners of my eyes. *Dammit, Lash. Now you're just embarrassing yourself.* My voice shook. "It was just good knowing I wasn't alone."

Kellan leaned forward, put his hand on mine, gazing at me with quiet concern. "Lashka, I spoke to security while you were in the jacks, and that gobshite is being removed from the premises. So you don't have to worry about him again."

I nodded, still not trusting myself to speak.

The waiter distracted me by setting fresh drinks on the table. "*Les calmars, s'il vous plait.*" Kellan's French was passable.

I raised my glass to Kellan. "To having friends in a fight."

He clinked my glass, then studied me over the rim of his. "I should probably apologize for my behavior yesterday. There was a bit of a crisis at work, but that's not really an excuse for rudeness."

Who was this person and what had he done with Mr. Grumpy? Although I had to say I preferred the new Kellan. He definitely looked more relaxed today, lounging in perfectly fitted jeans and a white cotton shirt with rolled up sleeves, unbuttoned at the neck—the effortlessly casual look that many men tried to pull off but that Kellan owned with ease. His hair still looked roguishly disheveled, dark tendrils framing his cheeks and hanging down over one eye. Had I not been pretty sure he was a businessman, I would have taken him for a model.

But it was his eyes that really marked the change. They

were a dark grey, and yesterday, would barely meet mine—so little that I hadn't even noticed their color. But tonight he watched me attentively, to the point where I started to feel a little self-conscious.

Our calamari arrived. My mouth watered and my stomach growled. I hadn't eaten anything except that salad since breakfast. Kellan ordered us a few more tapas-like dishes, not even bothering with a menu—locally cured meats like ham prisuttu and figatellu sausages, a shareable portion of *civet de sanglier*, and tasters of azimu seafood soup—and paired the lot with a full-bodied Bordeaux. He was right, the food was excellent. He had an annoying habit of being right about a lot of things.

Our dinner conversation couldn't be called scintillating, but Kellan deliberately kept to light topics like the local food, suggesting a couple of restaurants I might want to check out, and a few sights to visit if I ventured further afield than Porto-Vecchio.

We'd reached the cheese stage of the evening, and he waved over the bartender. "*Deux verres de mirto, s'il vous plait.*"

The bartender disappeared and came back with two shot glasses filled with a clear liquid.

I eyed them doubtfully. "I'm not really into grappa." Firewater wasn't my thing.

Kellan lifted his glass, amused. "Try it. I promise you you've never tasted anything like it."

I picked up the glass and sniffed. It had a light, slightly medicinal scent. I took a tentative sip. "Oh!" The drink was not harsh at all—sweet but not cloyingly so, with spicy overtones.

"It's made from *baies de myrte*, a myrtle berry found only in the maquis. I thought you might like it."

Right *again*. "I do."

We sipped our digestifs in companionable silence. Maybe conversation was overrated.

The stars came out in a twinkling canopy. The low rumble of surf sounded from the ocean in the distance. I basked in the warm glow of my alcohol buzz and a sated stomach. But finally I had to admit to myself I was procrastinating. Despite Kellan's assurances and his unexpectedly pleasant company given our rough start, a part of me had stayed so long because I really didn't want to risk running into Nick on one of the garden paths on my way back to my room. But I did have work to do tomorrow.

"I should go." But I didn't get up.

Kellan gave me a measuring look. "Would you like me to walk you to your room?"

"I—that would be great. I know you said he'd be gone, but …"

"It's fine. Let me get *l'addition*."

"I think dinner's on me tonight."

"Nonsense. There's no need to thank me."

I laughed. "First, yes there is. But second, I think the hotel's comping me my bill tonight." I explained about the air conditioning.

"Ah. Then I accept your generous offer."

We stood, and I confirmed the arrangement with the bartender on the way out, but made sure I added a tip to my room's bill. Kellan escorted me outside and down the pathway, past the deep turquoise glow of the pool and down the stairs towards our rooms.

I couldn't help peering suspiciously at the faces of the few other guests we passed. "I hate how that douche harshed a perfectly good vibe. I hate that he's still lurking in the back of my mind." How he'd always be.

"Guys like that hate women. Have no idea how to treat them."

"Too many guys don't."

"That's a bit of an overgeneralization, don't you think?"

"The problem is, walking home in the dark like this, if I was by myself and ran into you, and didn't know you, I can't tell if you're a Nick or a nice guy. And the risk that you might be a Nick means I always, *always* have to be on guard."

"He's not here anymore."

"Not at the resort, no. But I could still bump into him in town. I once got run out of Chamonix by a guy I met. We weren't even intimate. We got into a minor fender-bender trying to find a party, and he blamed me for it even though I was sitting in his passenger seat. When I refused to pay him for the damage, he started stalking me. It was just easier to run, because he scared me so badly—came up to me at a restaurant, started raging, and threw a glass of water in my face—that I had to get my friends to escort me out of town. I've never been back to Chamonix again." Although I did have some other *very* fond memories of my time there. "Too many guys are assholes to women, and too few other guys call them out on it."

"What I hear you saying is that you can't trust any man who makes a pass at you."

I rolled my eyes. "Don't be obtuse. An unsolicited, unwelcome pass when I'm minding my own business maybe. I do actually date, you know. Successfully." I rounded on him. "You were impatient for me to follow you down that trail, yesterday, but that was the calculus that was going through my mind when I hesitated. You were a complete unknown, and I've met too many Nicks. But now that I've spent some time with you, I feel fairly confident I wouldn't have to stiff-arm you if you made a pass at me and I said no."

"You're not ready for the kind of pass I'd make at you."

"I beg your pardon?" I'd had similar discussions with a few male acquaintances but this was a new rhetorical move.

He shrugged. "You're not ready. Not tonight."

"Don't patronize me." Why did guys always think they knew more about what I was ready for than I did?

We had reached his villa. His nostrils flared. "Never mind. I don't need this." He spun on his heel and disappeared into the building, leaving me standing on the path. The door clicked shut.

"No. Uh-*uh*." I'd had it with this bullshit. I marched up to the door and rapped on it with my knuckles. I kept hitting it until Kellan flung the door open and glowered at me from the stoop, framed beneath the heavy stone lintel. I stuck out my chin. "Out with it. You have something you want to say? A move you want to make? Bring it."

He stared at me for the space of three breaths. Then he stepped forward. His arm snaked up, his palm clasping my nape and tugging me to him. His mouth covered mine.

I stiffened in shock, pressed a hand to his chest. My lips parted in surprise, and he wasted no time, probing deeply with his tongue. Then he sucked in a breath, drawing my tongue into his mouth, as if he would swallow me whole.

He withdrew from the kiss—his fingers still searing the back of my neck—ran his nose along my cheek, his mouth along my jaw line. His breath thrummed hot in my ear. His voice growled low, each syllable enunciated with merciless deliberation. "I want you. I want to fuck you, my lovely, until you forget how to form words." He pressed his hips to mine to let me feel just how prepared he was to back up those words. "Is that plain enough?"

He released my nape, fixing me with a stare like a hunting panther, close enough to still feel his warmth but not touching me at all. It was crude, in some ways cruder than Nick, but it was *nothing* like Nick. I stood rooted to the spot, almost panting, unable to look away.

"Stay." He shrugged. "Or go. But choose. Now."

The moment hung in the balance, all my muscles tensed like a doe poised to spring away. My chest heaved, and heat flared across my skin. I could still taste the barest hint of the myrtle. He never took his eyes from mine. Didn't say another word, the laconic bastard.

Then the corner of his mouth curved upwards in the slightest smile, his gaze filled with a knowing, burning intent, and I knew I was lost.

26

CHAPTER THREE

HE stayed still as cat ready to pounce, every muscle taut, waiting, patient. He'd made my choice clear, and wouldn't make it for me.

I lifted an unsteady hand, placed it against his flank. His chest rose and fell rhythmically beneath my palm. I spread my fingers and the cloth of his cotton shirt shifted against his ribs.

I leaned the tiniest bit forward. Tilted my head.

Grazed his throat with my nose, the barest hint of my lips.

Offered him my neck.

The dam of his stillness broke. His arms enveloped me, one hand tangling in the waves of my hair, the other at the small of my back, his mouth clamped against the hollow behind my jaw as his tongue traced lines of fire up to my ear. He swung me across the threshold, hipchecked the door shut, and pushed me up against it.

Now his mouth devoured mine, his kisses deep, rough,

urgent. I ground my hips against his in answer, my hands stroking his shoulder blades, enjoying the play of his muscles beneath my fingers. Behind the barrier of our clothes, his cock throbbed. I'd suddenly never wanted anything more, undone by the rush of my desire. I reached for his belt.

He had other ideas.

He slid his hands down my waist and beneath the elastic of my skirt and panties. He paused to stroke and squeeze my buttocks, and my glutes bunched as I pressed back into his grip. Then he knelt, sweeping my clothing down with him. The cool AC on my exposed skin did nothing to soothe the heat along the path of his palms.

He ran his tongue along the inside of one thigh, the stubble on his chin scraping and his long silken locks tickling my skin in its wake. I lifted my feet to step out of my underwear, my core tightening and twitching, anticipating the advance of his mouth. His hand folded around my ankle, the top of his head brushing against my mound.

His fingers grazed my calf, then he placed his hand under my knee and raised it to rest my leg on his shoulder. He looked up at me then, a wordless question in his bottomless eyes.

The cautious voice inside my head that was asking me what the hell I thought I was doing got shouted down by the sheer ferocity of my lust. My gaze drifted from Kellan's eyes, down his strong nose, to his full parted lips. What I craved from that lush mouth didn't involve words or thought or questions of any kind.

I threaded my fingers through the hair at the top of his head and pulled him to me in answer, splayed the fingers of my other hand against the door. Arched my back in pleasure as his hot breath swathed my thighs and his lips made first contact with my cunt, already slick and engorged with need.

He brought his hands up to support and massage my ass as he buried his mouth between my lower lips. His tongue circled slowly around my hole, learning the lay of the land, and I let out an involuntary gasp.

He speared me with his tongue and I bucked. His hands pulled me closer and I lost track of everything but the burning contours of his mouth and the flicking of his tongue, slicking, lapping, burrowing, soft and yet so, so powerful. I pumped my hips as his lips massaged me, pressing myself to the wall, trying to escape from and meld with him at the same time. Small noises emerged from the back of my throat.

He found my clit, fluttered his tongue against it, teasing. I clutched his hair as tingling waves spread out through my belly. His tongue circled the nub, slowly, slowly, as I bucked again, moaning. Then he pursed his lips and sucked hard, building a rhythm of pressure, release, pressure, release, torment and rapture, until I could endure no more and I cried out, shuddering and writhing in an exquisite climax.

I leaned against the door, panting, collecting the tattered shreds of my self-possession. Finally I eased my leg off Kellan's shoulder, my other leg shaking from the strain of holding me up. I braced myself on his shoulders and took several long, deep breaths while he planted languid, open-mouthed kisses along my hip crease and belly. What those lips lacked in conversational skills, they made up for in dexterity. In spades.

"What just happened?" I whispered hoarsely. The speed of it all dizzied me.

Kellan lifted my blouse and exhaled reproachfully on my navel. "You're still talking."

He rose, unbuttoning his shirt, and shrugged it off, using it to scrub his face before tossing it aside. He had a sleekly fit look, his arms and torso tautly muscled instead of bulky, with a light dusting of chest hair, and a narrow waist and broad shoulders.

Before I could take more time to admire his physique, he stooped and kissed my throat, grabbed my wrist, and pressed my palm to the front of his jeans. I pushed against the bulge, massaging his crotch as he undulated his hips. He unbuttoned my blouse, then stroked my shoulders as he slid it down, nibbling a line from my neck to my shoulder as he exposed more skin. I reached for his belt with my other hand, but he blocked me, pinning my hand against the wall.

"Not yet."

He unhooked my bra and freed my breasts, giving each one a slow perusal with his mouth and tongue. He cupped one, squeezed, and drew the nipple slowly into his mouth, fluttering his tongue along the tip. I inhaled sharply.

He slid his hands down to my ass, gripped it, then lifted me up. I took the hint and wrapped my legs around his back and my arms around his neck, burying my nose in his hair, which smelled of vanilla. Bracing me against the wall, he kissed my breasts again, nipping gently on each nipple. Then he shifted his grip on me, making sure of his hold, and carried me to the sofa, where he knelt on the cushions, leaned forward and almost tenderly laid me down.

I sprawled against the cushions, wondering just what, exactly, I'd gotten myself into, but not really complaining. I hadn't had an orgasm like that in far too long. This man had gone from irascible to lustful in the blink of an eye, but despite his taciturn demeanor, and unlike the asshole at the bar, he actually seemed to like women. And this woman in particular, though between the sick bag and my pestering, I couldn't quite fathom why.

My thoughts returned to the fucking at hand, and I found him studying me, raking his eyes along my body, drinking me in. If a look could make me come, that might be it. His grey eyes, shrouded by a stray wave of hair, gave nothing, and yet everything away, his expression both thoughtful and sly.

"What shall I do with you next?" he murmured.

He fixed me with that stare of his, and unbuckled his belt. I swallowed. He stepped out of his jeans, and slipped off his boxers, his cock springing free. He frowned in irritation. "Don't move." I took in his sculpted thighs and calves, the ripple of muscle along his abs as he twisted, searching for something. He looked around the room, located his messenger bag, and withdrew a condom wrapper—I guess it paid to travel prepared—while I admired his perfectly formed ass.

He stood and deliberately took his time sheathing himself, letting me think long and hard about what was coming. Heat swept over me again as his fingers flexed and clasped his shaft. He rubbed himself, drawing out the wait, and gave me a crooked smile when he saw me squirm with impatience. One of my hands moved to caress my breast, and I slipped two fingers between my thighs, trying to ease the inexorable pressure in my loins.

He watched me, eyes hooded, clearly enjoying my discomfiture, and in turn I couldn't take my eyes from his strong hands sliding up and down the length I ached to have inside me.

Finally he came to the sofa and crawled onto it, his knees to either side of my waist. He clasped my wrists, brought the hand I'd been using to salve myself to his lips and sucked the fingers clean. Then he repositioned my arms, pinning them over my head. He gazed into my eyes, his thick black mane hanging down, framing his face. He looked at me like that for what felt like forever, not doing anything, just searing me with his gaze, never taking his eyes from mine.

I found myself breathing harder, my nostrils flaring, desperate for more air as the naked desire on his face sucked all the oxygen from the space around us. No one had *ever* looked at me quite like this, and a flurry of panic knotted in my belly. I tensed my wrists, testing his will. He put the tiniest bit more pressure into his grip.

I'd never felt more vulnerable.

I'd never felt more wanted.

I inhaled deeply, and let out a lingering, shaky breath. Did it again. Did it again, and again, until I lay calm and open beneath his piercing gaze.

Finally, he leaned down, rested his cheek against my temple, his hair brushing my forehead, his mouth at my ear. "Good," he breathed. "Now you know, my lovely, how much I want you. And I *will* have you. All of you, body and soul. Won't I?" He nuzzled my ear. "Because you'll give yourself to me."

I had never been more turned on in my life.

He released my hands, withdrew from my ear, and grazed my brow with his lips, tracing a line back down along my cheek, delicate and soft, feather light. He did the same on the other side, finding all the planes of my face, the bridge of my nose, the line of my jaw, before stopping, his nose not quite touching mine, hovering, waiting again. He was so close his eyes filled my whole field of vision. Our breath mingled and my spine tingled along its whole length. I lay poised between lust and desire, and he was the only thing in my universe.

I stretched, ever so slightly, and bridged the infinitesimal gap he'd left between us, my lips brushing his.

He parted his lips, and pressed them softly to mine. His lips played with mine, the kisses light, almost chaste, as he lowered his body and stretched his entire length atop me. I welcomed the weight, his warmth, like a long-lost friend. He lifted his head, swept a hand across my forehead, tucking a stray strand of hair behind my ear. "Are you ready?" he whispered.

I nodded.

His cock pulsed against my mound. "Then let's begin."

He crushed his mouth to mine, suddenly rapacious, and I answered just as hungrily, opening wide and letting his tongue have its way with mine. I wanted him now like I'd never wanted anyone before. I tangled my fingers in his hair and clutched him to me, drinking him in, lapping him up, unable to get enough, desperate for more of him, more.

He slid his hand along my flank, slipped it between us, tested my cunt, found it soaking and ripe. I let my legs fall open, and he palmed me, coating his hand. He lifted his hips and grasped his cock, slicking it, but I batted his hand aside and raised my own hips, grasping his ass and grinding his pelvis into me, running the outside of my slit up and down the length of his shaft. He bit my neck and I squeezed his ass tighter. He growled, and once again reached for his cock, grasping it and circling my clit with its soft, soft tip.

I tilted my hips again, thrusting, impatient, trying to tell him how much I needed him inside me. He laughed softly. "In my own sweet time, my lovely." I whined in protest and he laughed again. "If you insist."

He guided himself to my hole, and probed the opening with the tip of his cock. I pulled his ass to me and he sank into my wet depths as I took the entire length of him inside me.

He paused there, and I closed my eyes, my body full of him, replete.

He eased back, gave a small thrust. I met him in kind. He thrust again, a longer stroke, and I arched my back. He ran his tongue along my collarbone and kissed my breast again, and thrust harder, deeper. I clutched his buttocks, pulling him in, in.

With each stroke, the rhythm built, like waves crashing against a stormy shore. I felt my own wave building, and sought out his mouth with mine, wanting as much of him inside me as I could find. He thrusts came quick and urgent now and I writhed and shuddered.

And then he pulled back, didn't start the next thrust, his tip just still inside me. I moaned in protest. He slammed into me once, hard, and I cried out. He pulled back again. Waited three breaths. Pounded me once again. I gasped. He smashed me again, and then in the space between thrusts, reached down and thumbed my overstimulated clit. I screamed as great, shuddering waves of pleasure crashed over and around me and he thrust into me again, and again, and again until he came in his own bucking climax.

He collapsed on top of me and I just lay beneath him, one hand stroking his back. With the other, I smoothed back his tousled hair and stared up at him in wonder. I stretched up and kissed him, softly, gratefully.

He slid out of me and eased his body to the side, sitting up slowly, stroking my flank.

"I'll be right back." He disappeared deeper into the villa, returning with towels and a wash cloth, having disposed of his condom.

"Come with me. I'll clean you off." He took my hand, and pulled me up from the couch. Instead of heading for the bathroom, he padded out to the villa's private patio, past a spa I eyed wistfully, and into an outdoor shower surrounded by the local tumbled-stone and wood privacy screens.

A cool breeze swept in from the ocean, soothing my fevered skin. He set the taps, testing the water, and once satisfied with the temperature, tugged me beneath the stream. I tilted my face up to the spray, letting the water sluice the perspiration of our lovemaking away. He picked up the wash cloth and sponged my skin, making slow strokes down my back, along my arms, around to my stomach, finishing by cleaning between my legs with a gentle rub.

"Thank you," I murmured dazedly.

He shook his head with regret. "*Still* talking."

He tossed the face cloth away, spun me round and pinned my wrists to the wooden wall of the shower enclosure, his breath coming hot against the back of my neck, his whole body pressed against me, taut with intent.

My breath hitched. "I can't. I'm not ready."

"Don't fret, my lovely," he snarled softly, and my knees went weak. "I'll make sure you're ready."

"What about a sheath?" I offered as my final delaying tactic, though my traitorous body was already aroused by the thought of what might come next.

"Did you think I came back from the jacks with my hands empty?" He leaned away, reaching for something near the towels, then held a foil-wrapped disk in my field of view. He tore it open and put it on.

He enfolded me completely in his arms, one hand fondling my breast, the other exploring my cunt. He pushed me against the wall with his whole body, the entire length of his shaft wedged along the crack of my ass. He ground his hips lightly against my buttocks and licked the back of my neck, moving up until he tongued my ear. Helpless desire overtook me again and I squeezed my ass against his hips as he slid his hand up to my throat, turning my head so he could ravish my mouth with his.

All the while his other hand worked patiently, one finger sliding in and out of me, the others slicking my folds as I whimpered with a need I had thought exhausted. His cock twitched against me. I writhed against it, and he groaned. Suddenly he pulled his hips away. I bent my ass back, reaching and bereft at the sudden loss of his skin against mine. Then the tip of his cock probed my cunt. He slid his penis along my labia, teasing, and I tilted my pelvis, desperate to engulf him. He guided himself in, slowly, satisfying himself that he'd indeed made me ready.

I sighed as he filled me. He entwined his fingers with mine and pinned my hand against the wall. With the other, he played with my clit. His first, deep thrust met my own, then with the pressure of his palm on my mound he hugged me tight to him, giving me quick, hard thrusts that left me gasping.

As the water cascaded down our backs, he took me, took everything, and true to his promise, the ocean breeze carried the scent of night jasmine and my inchoate cries out into the darkness.

CHAPTER FOUR

I woke with a heavy languid weight in my limbs, my head in the crook of Kellan's shoulder, one arm flung across his torso, a leg splayed over his thighs. My tanned skin stood out starkly against his pale Irish white. I lay still in the bed, warm and complete in the half-circle of his arm. Our chests rose and fell in an intimate syncopation. His finger traced idle whorls on my shoulder. His breath stirred the hair on the top of my head. The light of full day streamed in through the window wall.

"Good morning," he said.

I shifted slightly so I could look up at him. Opened my mouth to reply, then shut it with a click.

Kellan chuckled, then pressed his mouth to the top of my head. "Speak. You're safe now." He leaned away to eye me speculatively. "Unless you'd like another go?"

My skin flushed at the mere thought and my clit pulsed. "Mmmm." I toyed with his chest hair, stretched my neck, and tongued his nipple. "I might, at that." I reached down and palmed his cock, then tickled his balls.

"You, my lovely, are a marvel," he said hoarsely.

I slid up and draped my body over his. I kissed him, slow and deep, as he relaxed his jaw to draw my tongue fully in. I took my time, savoring him, inhaling his clean scent, twining my tongue with his. We explored each other's mouths, trading tastes, content for a while with this simple intimacy. He stroked his hands up and down my back, tracing the bumps of my spine. His cock hardened beneath my belly.

I sat up, straddling his thighs, reached into the nightstand, and withdrew another condom. I sheathed him with gentle deliberation, and massaged his shaft with slow sure strokes. He closed his eyes and groaned softly.

I moved up his thighs to straddle his hips and stomach, sliding my labia along the length of his cock. As my cunt grew wetter, I ground down harder. Kellan grunted, locking his gaze to mine, resting his hands lightly on my hips but not directing anything, letting me choreograph this time. I placed my palms on his shoulders, levered my hips up until his cock sprang up, then undulated until my hole found his tip. I sank down one slow breath at a time, never taking my eyes from his. I sat for a moment, not moving, enjoying the feeling of him filling me, watching me, waiting.

I clenched my vagina. Kellan hissed. I clenched again, and he inhaled sharply.

I rocked my hips back and forth, back and forth, not too fast, not too slow. Kellan cupped my ass, squeezing gently. I slid up and down the length of his cock in a leisurely rhythm.

I leaned over him, my hair brushing his cheeks, as I continued to pump my hips at an easy pace. "I could do this all day," I murmured into his ear before sitting back up, still rocking.

"Don't make promises you can't keep." He let go of my ass, flexed his knees, and using his hands, surged up to a seated position as well, almost slipping out of me, before going in even deeper. He hugged me close, and I wrapped my legs around his back. I arched my neck and he kissed the hollow of my throat, bent his head to my breast, circled his tongue around my aureola and took a long draw on my nipple.

I thrust against him harder, and now his hips pumped in time to mine. Stroke after stroke, I matched him beat for beat. His tongue coated my breast, his other hand clenched my ass, the base of his cock pounded my clit. We clutched each other, slick with sweat, each trying to drive deeper into the other.

I tangled the fingers of both hands in his thick hair, reveling in the feel of it feathering against my chest, keeping his mouth clamped to my breast as he sucked and lapped at my nipple. I slammed into him, and squeezed the muscles of my vagina again.

He gave a muffled grunt and bucked against me, and his release pulsed against my inner walls.

We sat quietly for a moment, both breathing as though we'd done a mile-long run along the beach. He hugged me close. Nuzzled my shoulder as he slid out of me, spent.

I unwrapped my legs from around him and swung them

over the edge of the bed, but he gripped my hand, preventing me from getting up. "We're not *quite* finished here." He slipped off the bed, pushed me back onto it, then knelt on the floor, putting both my knees over his shoulders. He grabbed my hips, slid me forward, and then sucked me off until I clenched the sheets and cried out, arching and quaking.

I lay staring at the ceiling, my mind a blank. A very satisfied blank.

He ducked out from under my legs, sat against the edge of the bed. "Penny for your thoughts."

"Oh, *now* you want to hear them." I propped myself up so I could see him.

He gave me a wicked grin. The man could actually smile. I liked the creases around his eyes when he smiled.

"I was just wondering how in the space of twenty-four hours the irritating curmudgeon I met on my first day here could turn into the most attentive lover I've ever had."

"This place is good at clearing my head, which is why I come here." His hand stroked my calf. "I hadn't counted on such a thorough distraction, though. I have a bit of a weakness for women who know what they want." He squeezed my knee, then stood up. "Why don't you get freshened up while I order us some breakfast."

I padded into the bathroom and ran myself a long, hot shower, then toweled off my hair and wrapped myself in one of the hotel's terry-cloth robes. When I returned to the bedroom, the murmur of Kellan's voice on the phone drifted in from the other room. The package he'd received at reception upon arrival was open on the dresser. I hadn't noticed it when we'd tumbled into the darkened room last night. Brochures for the Conlan Vienna lay scattered beside it.

I frowned. I flipped over the box's flap, took a look at the packing slip. "Christopher Conlan, c/o Conlan Corsica Resort."

Slow dawning horror prickled up my spine. I went out to the living room, where my lover was just hanging up the phone. He'd thrown on some clothes.

"I thought you said your name was Kellan."

"It is. Kellan is my middle name. I use it because otherwise people confuse me with my father, Christopher Conlan Sr."

I put my hand to my mouth. "Oh god." I looked around, frantically searching out my clothes. "I need to leave."

"Lashka, what's wrong?"

"What's *wrong*?" I snatched up my skirt, blouse, and underwear from the floor by the door. "You're Chris Conlan, for fuck's sake. You own this hotel. And *I* work for Pritchard, Hanson & Vale. You know, the people who want to buy it? The people who have a very strict fraternization policy between employees and stakeholders."

He reached out to try to get me to face him, but I shook him off and slipped my feet into my wedges. "Lashka, I'm sure we can explain to them—"

I turned to him, my eyes brimming. "They're going to fire me. I can't be here. I should never have been here." I clutched

my clothes to the robe, grabbed my purse, and darted out the
door.

"Lashka!"

I ran down the path to my suite, but the clutter in my
purse stymied me as I rummaged around for my keycard.
Kellan—no, Chris—caught up to me at the entrance as I
fumbled to find it. This time he spun me around, keeping a
firm grip on my upper arms. "Lashka. Please don't leave. Not
like this. Not after …" He looked up at the sky, back at me. "I
want to see you again."

"I *can't*. However much I might want to." And I really,
really wanted to. "I have to go. You have to let me. I'm sorry."
I'd never been sorrier for anything.

His grey eyes bored into mine. Then he clasped my
cheeks between his palms and kissed me. He kissed me like
he was trying to burn the memory of my taste into his
tongue, rough and messy and desperate. He released me
slowly. I put my forehead to his chest.

"At least let me know what happens." He leaned his chin
on my hair, hugging me tight, then pressed a business card
into my palm.

I nodded, unable to speak, then stepped out of the
comfort of his arms. I entered my room and shut the door
with a click of empty finality, before sinking down to the
floor. I pressed the heels of my hands to my eyes and sobbed
until the tears wouldn't come anymore. Then I got up to pack
and change my flight.

CHAPTER FIVE

PRITCHARD, Hanson & Vale fired me on the spot. While they claimed they understood the circumstances after I'd explained myself, they refused to set aside their zero-tolerance policy. As they were still recovering from a major conflict-of-interest scandal that had nearly wiped them out, the optics of this threatened to set the cat among the shareholder pigeons again. For posterity, I emailed my boss the abbreviated report on the Conlan Corsica I'd written on the plane back to Montreal. Then I cleared out the few things I kept at the desk I hardly ever sat at, and left the building, thoroughly deflated.

The best job I'd ever had, and the best lover I'd ever had. Both gone in the blink of an eye.

In the two weeks since, I'd grown bored of sitting on my couch trawling job boards, trying to figure out how to spin getting terminated for cause to prospective employers.

Trying not to think about Kellan.

He'd asked me to call him, but each time I went to do it, I could only stare ambivalently at the phone. The conflict of interest had vanished with my job, so in theory there was nothing stopping us from seeing each other again. But I'd never experienced anything as intense as our night together. What if it had been a fluke?

I knew next to nothing about him, and aside from an unmistakable chemistry in bed, there was a distinct possibility that we were otherwise poorly matched.

He was a very rich man, and I was nothing but an unemployed peon. He was probably having second thoughts too. After all, he had a phone too if he wanted to reach out. And he hadn't.

A part of me wanted to leave our night just as it was: a perfect memory that I'd savor forever.

Another part of me wondered just what the hell I thought I was doing, moping here by myself.

This was pointless. I hauled on my jogging gear and went for a run to work off my frustration.

My phone rang as I reached the promenade by the Lachine canal, the call display showing an unfamiliar European number. My pulse hitched. Normally I'd chalk it up to a telemarketer or scammer, and ignore it, but decided to answer. If it was a scammer I'd take out my frustrations on them. But maybe it was Kellan. "Yes?"

"Lashka Wright?" A woman's voice. Dammit.

"Yes."

"I'm Liliane DeGroot. I represent the Task Agency. Your name came up recently as being of potential interest to a client of ours. Would you be free to meet them? This evening?"

I stopped in the middle of the path so I wouldn't sound out of breath. "Whereabouts?"

"The client is staying at the Opal Vieux-Montréal and would like to chat over dinner."

"As long as it's at the restaurant and not their room." Mealtime interviews were a little unusual for me, and I didn't need a MeToo moment in addition to everything else that had happened.

"Most certainly. The concierge will be expecting you."

"May I ask how you came to hear about me?"

"I'm afraid I'm not at liberty to divulge that information."

Sometimes I hated the games recruiters played. But I didn't have very many options at the moment. "Can you at least tell me the name of the client?"

"You'll be meeting with Mister Edvard Kuiper." I suppressed a small sigh of disappointment. "I will let him explain what they're looking for in a new hire." She gave me a time and the address of the Opal, and bid me goodbye.

I glanced at the clock on my phone, working backwards. Still plenty of time to finish my jog, get cleaned up, and make my way downtown.

Things were looking up.

CHAPTER SIX

"Reservation for Kuiper?"

"Right this way." The maitre d' led me through the Opal's darkly paneled restaurant, to a discreet booth near the back.

Edvard Kuiper stood up as I arrived. "Punctuality. Always a good sign." He waved me into my seat and sat down across from me. "Please forgive the last-minute arrangements, Ms. Wright. I fly out to Prague tomorrow and this was the only slot I had available. A man has to eat, after all. Would you like a menu as well?"

We made light chitchat as we scanned our menus and ordered, and then Kuiper got down to business. "I'm the new Chief Operating Officer of the Opal chain of boutique hotels and resorts. Opal hired me because they're losing repeat customers and want to reverse that trend. You came highly recommended to me as someone who can spot some of the subtler issues that might be causing us to bleed customers. I'd like to bring you on to evaluate our worst-performing properties in such a manner that they don't know they're being assessed. Everyone knows how to put on a good show for management for an audit. I want the real story."

I blinked at Kuiper. This was right up my alley. "Contract or permanent employment?"

"Contract for now. Travel expenses fully paid, of course. You'd be quite busy over the next six months as we'd like to understand if it's a systemic problem or isolated to a few properties."

"Then let's do three weeks on, one week off." I found it really hard to recover from jet lag if I bounced around too constantly. "Would I report directly to you?"

"Yes. In fact, I don't want anyone else knowing I've hired you, as I don't want to risk compromising secrecy here. You'll be off the books, so to speak."

"I'm very discreet."

"So I've been led to believe."

"May I ask by whom?"

"Kellan Conlan gave me your name."

Huh.

"Is that a problem?"

"No. Not at all. I hadn't realized he thought that highly of me." Professionally speaking.

Our food arrived and Kuiper told me a bit more about the Opal Group and his goals for the company. He asked me about how I worked and what kind of reports I produced. I used the time to probe my potential new boss on his working methods and style. I liked what I saw: Kuiper seemed knowledgeable about the industry, while possessing a frank, no-nonsense manner. We ended the evening with his promise to send me a contract to look over in the morning. He expected an answer from me by the end of the week, but I suspected I wouldn't need that long to come to a decision.

He escorted me to the lobby. As we shook hands, he looked over my shoulder. "Ah, Conlan. I was wondering if we might see you here."

"Liliane told me where I could find you." Kellan appeared from around my shoulder, and shook Kuiper's hand. I shunted aside thoughts of how Kellan's hands had played me like a fine instrument, the silky warmth of them against my skin. Draping myself over my reference was the wrong way to end an interview.

"I really must thank you for your recommendation. Ms. Wright is indeed very impressive, but I expected no less from one of your referrals."

"Lashka's an exceptional find."

Based on the heat that bloomed across my cheeks, I must have flushed a vivid shade of scarlet.

"Would you like to have a drink?" Kuiper asked.

"Actually, I was hoping to steal Ms. Wright from you. We have some other business to conclude."

Conclude. That sounded pretty final. Oh well. I smiled at Kuiper, even as I braced for near-term disappointment. "I look forward to seeing those documents."

"It was a pleasure meeting you, Ms. Wright. I hope I'll have reason to be seeing more of you soon." Kuiper headed for the elevator, leaving me trying not to stare awkwardly at Kellan.

"Come with me?" he asked. "I'd like to show you something." He led me out the back of the Opal's lobby, to the entrance on the block it backed onto, then across the street. We walked into the sleek metal and glass lobby of the new Conlan Quintessence, a set of suites and luxury townhomes. He called an elevator, swiped his card and hit the button for the penthouse, and said nothing as the car whooshed us up.

I couldn't read his expression, couldn't tell if he was angry, disappointed, or something else. But I knew better than to make a smart-ass comment right now.

The elevator opened right into the suite. Or maybe it was an apartment. I knew that some of the rooms here were condos, while others were standard hotel rooms. The city spread out beneath us behind the floor-to-ceiling glass windows, Mont-Royal to the northwest.

Kellan walked straight out to the large rooftop patio, letting me trail behind him. Still no words. *Le plus ça change,* apparently. He leaned against the railing, gazing out at the view, the river and Old Montreal to one side, downtown skyscrapers behind and to our right. A few cars honked in the canyons of the streets, and I thought I discerned the clop of a horse pulling a calèche.

"Is this what you wanted to show me?" I finally asked after at least ninety seconds of continuing silence. It *was* a spectacular view.

He waved a dismissive hand. "That was just an excuse to get you up here." He turned to face me, one hip still against the railing. "PHV contacted me directly, you know. Apologizing for their employee's *behavior*." He sniffed derisively. "I canceled the deal, but not before I demanded to see your report. I'm sorry for unwittingly putting you in that position. Kuiper's good. He used to work for me until Opal poached him, and he immediately came to mind when I heard what happened. You can trust him." He shook his head, stared out at the city again. "You never called."

"I—no."

"May I ask why?" His tone was casual but his eyes were anything but.

"Because …" I glanced away, met his gaze again. We had been so physically open with each other. I owed him more openness now. "Because I was afraid."

"Of me?"

"No. Of course not." I wasn't sure how to put it. "That what happened … wasn't real. That it was too good to be true. That we could never … never recapture whatever that was." I took a breath. "It was so …"

He raised an eyebrow.

I made a small noise of frustration, then said the thing that had been lurking at the back of my mind these past couple of weeks, that I hadn't wanted to look at too closely. "I think … I think you might have ruined me for anyone else." I couldn't imagine wanting anybody else's hands on me after experiencing his touch. "And I don't know what to do. I wasn't ready for that. I wasn't looking for it."

He stared at me, the silence stretching out. "Do you not wish to pursue this, then? If that's what you want, you can walk out of here right now and never hear from me again."

I swallowed.

He stepped in closer. "Because I do. Just say the word, Lashka, and I will pursue you to the ends of the Earth."

How did he do it? How did he sweep all my doubts aside with a penetrating look and a few words?

I launched myself across the intervening space between us, grabbed his collar in my fists, and pulled his mouth down to mine, my need for him once again complete and all-consuming. He grunted, clasped my face in his hands, and we each drank the other in. His taste and clean scent flooded across my senses, my kisses frantic, urgent.

"You don't need—" One kiss. "—to pursue me." Another kiss. I circled his tongue with mine. "Just take me." I ground my hips against his pelvis. "I'm yours. Take me now."

I tore at his belt, unclasped the buckle, my fingers working hungrily at the button and zip of his fly, all the while massaging his crotch. He growled in my ear, buried his nose in my hair. Then he pushed me up against the railing and rucked up my skirt. He slid his hand inside my panties, his fingers finding me already wet and slick with the intensity of my lust. I ground against his palm. He worked my underwear down my thighs, and I shimmied and wriggled against him until they fell free. I pushed his pants and boxers down until his shaft sprang free.

"Condom," I husked.

"Here." He whipped one out of his breast pocket, and I made short work of making him safe.

He cupped my ass, then ran his hand along the underside of one thigh, caressing, lifting. I hooked my leg over his hip, took his cock and slid it between my legs, riding its whole length along my slit, until he was just as wet as me.

I exhaled a light "ha" as he entered me. I brushed the hair from his brow and looked into those eyes grey as storm clouds, my own filled with wonder and trust. And a deep, endless desire. For him. For all of him.

"Kellan …" I bit my lip as he thrust deep. His mouth and teeth harrowed my throat, his stubble burning against my feverish skin. I pumped against him, met each thrust with one of my own. "Harder." I clutched at his ass and urged him on, my voice hoarse now. "Harder." My back arched, and as he claimed me, took me with swift, furious thrusts, a deep fullness spread out from my loins and I came in a great, shuddering surge, crying out his name as he bucked against me, his own orgasm pulsing within me.

We stood there wrapped in each other for few moments, my head resting against his chest, his hand stroking my back, both of us breathing like blown horses. He slid out of me and I kissed the hollow where his collarbones met.

"You fine, fine thing," he whispered against my hair. "Truly, my lovely."

I looked up at him. "Did you really cancel the whole deal?"

The laugh lines around his eyes creased in amusement. "Of course I did. The way those fuckers handled the whole affair pissed me off, throwing you under the bus like that. Besides …"

He stroked his knuckles along my cheek. "How could I possibly sell the place where I met you?"

I traced his dark eyebrows with my finger, marveling at how this man—gruff silences, fervent, loving intensity and all—had changed my life so swiftly, and how little I minded.

Then I sealed his statement with a long, lingering kiss.

Sweet DECEIT

CHAPTER ONE

THE bass thumped in my sternum, a counterpoint to my heartbeat. I shouted at Amélie to make myself heard. "You know I'm straight, right?"

Amélie laughed while her girlfriend Chloë nuzzled her ear. "But of course! We didn't think you'd mind coming here, though. You said you weren't *sur le marché*. No one will harass you here, so dance all you like. The men in other bars can sometimes be grabby."

All around us, stylish couples of all shapes, sizes, and gender mixes grooved to the trendiest tracks of the month in one of Paris's premier gay bars, whose name had slipped my wine-addled brain as soon as Amélie suggested it after our late dinner. I *had* in fact told her I was off the market for the moment. It might seem counterintuitive to come to the City of Love looking for a break from dating, but it was far from home, nobody knew me, and the job I'd displaced myself for consumed most of my time, spare or otherwise. Nobody knew or cared to hassle me about my self-imposed single status, and that suited me just fine.

I followed Amélie and Chloë as they wove through the crowd in search of the bar. Strobes flashed and glitter sparkled. An attractive woman in a pixie cut shimmied up to me but backed off when I smiled and gently shook my head. Boundaries respected. Nice.

Chloë ordered a round of shooters and I went for a whiskey sour. We slugged back the shots, then grabbed our highballs and found a counter to lean on, free tables being an endangered species. I spent a few minutes admiring the various dance moves on display while Amélie and Chloë had a good snog. If I was feeling brave, I might just not embarrass myself on the dance floor.

I'd almost finished my drink when a tall man came between Amélie and Chloë, interrupting their affections. "*C'est qui votre petite amie?*"

"Luc!" Amélie squealed. "*Quel surprise! Je te présente, Nadia.* Nadia, this is Luc."

I shook the hand he offered me as he leaned around Chloë. He was wearing a dark, V-neck T-shirt and faded-black slim-cut jeans. I still hadn't figured out how French men— and the women for that matter—managed to exude style in such simple attire. It must be the cut, which emphasized all the right aspects of his leanly muscled physique, broad shoulders, and well-defined arms. Several of the nearby men were checking him out. I didn't blame them.

"*C'est une collègue! Du Canada.*" Amélie shouted. We worked together at the Appropriated Art Society and Amélie had taken it upon herself to ensure my Paris experience was, well, Parisian.

Luc shrugged. "*Enchanté. On danse?*"

Chloë, not one to miss an opportunity for fun, took his hand and scurried out onto the dance floor. Amélie and I pushed through the throng after them and soon our little group was rocking out. I let the music take me over. I'd forgotten the last time I'd been to a club, the feel of the bass throbbing in my chest, the press of people close, the heat and miasma of perfume and alcohol and pheromones. Luc took turns with all us women, and I did a little bump and grind with both him and Chloë. What's a little exhibitionism among friends?

Luc sidled up behind Amélie and wrapped his arms around her. They swayed to the beat. It was clear from their easy physicality that they'd been friends a long time. Chloë sashayed up to them both and sandwiched Amélie between herself and Luc, giving Amélie a long kiss. Luc looked at me over Amélie's head and grinned. "Maybe we should find these two a room, *hein?*"

Amélie swatted his thigh and extricated herself from the dual embrace. "*Salaud!*" But she was smiling. "It is not a bad suggestion, though. This place is very loud. Why don't we go someplace more quiet for a drink?"

"I'm only a few blocks from here, and I found that wine you recommended. Why don't you all come back to my place?" I said.

We tumbled out of the club and staggered down the

street. The combined alcohol from the bar and the wine at dinner fuzzed my brain with a gentle euphoria.

Luc ambled by my side. "You are new to Paris?" Pah-ree. Like it was supposed to be pronounced.

"I've been here four months now."

"And you are with Amélie at the AAS?"

I nodded. The painstaking work involved enormous amounts of research on the provenance of looted artworks. But it was immensely rewarding to see a work lost in war returned to its rightful owners. The internship was the last stage of my PhD in art history, with the added benefit that living here was shoring up my middling French-language skills quite nicely.

"I can see why you might want to party," Luc said drily. "No girlfriend?"

"Oh, I'm not gay."

"*Pas de chum, d'abord?*"

"A boyfriend would just slow me down." After my last breakup, I'd sworn off men indefinitely.

"*Dommage.* A girl like you … all alone." Although Luc wasn't really paying attention to me. He'd turned to admire the retreating butt of a tall, darkly stubbled, and handsome man clearly heading for the club we'd just departed.

I elbowed Luc gently. "Sure you don't want to stay?"

"*Non, non.* Your wine sounded delightful."

Six minutes later, I unlocked the lobby door to my apartment and waved my friends inside. I tottered in after them and stopped dead.

"Darling! There you are. Finally. I've been waiting for hours."

I gaped in utter confusion at the grey-haired woman perched on a suitcase on the marble floor. My good mood vanished in an instant. "Mom?"

CHAPTER TWO

"WHAT are you doing here?" I stared at Mom, dumbfounded.

She peered at me through her progressive lenses. "What? I can't come and surprise my own daughter?"

No. Just no, Mom. There was a reason I'd chosen an internship a full continent and ocean away from my family. Her question expertly twisted the guilt knife in my gut, though.

"Some welcome mat you roll out."

"Mom! Seriously, why are you here?" She had better have a really good reason because this was not a pleasant surprise.

"Your father went to the evangelical ministers' convocation. I couldn't stay in the house alone any longer." Amélie, Chloë, and Luc all shifted uncomfortably.

"So you hopped a flight to Paris?" A spur-of-the-moment trip to Europe from the West Coast couldn't have been cheap, and my parents weren't exactly rolling in cash. "What about Aunt Liz?"

"She's in Hawaii." Why, oh why couldn't Mom have

picked Hawaii? The flight was shorter. "Besides, I've never been to Paris. We'll have a great old time. You'll hardly notice me at all. But I absolutely *must* meet that boyfriend you've been writing about."

Now it was my turn to shift uncomfortably. Fuck. There was no way I could produce said boyfriend, because I'd made him up. Conjured him out of my imagination so my mother would stop making snide remarks about my looming spinsterhood. Our fictitious "parting" at the end of my internship would have left me heartbroken, and given me another six months respite from further prodding and matchmaking. Sometimes it's easier to lie to family than put up with their endless nitpicking.

But now the game was up, my plan shot to hell because my mother couldn't just stay in her own lane.

Amélie nudged me. "You've been hiding a man from me? *Mais ça ne va pas*, Nadia? You know how I love the gossip."

I winced. Tried to buy time. "Exactly. I didn't tell you because … I'm … kind of private, in case you hadn't noticed."

Mom knew me too well and wasn't having any of it. "He doesn't exist, does he, Nadia?"

"No, he—"

Luc's arm snaked around my waist. "But of *course* I exist!" He gave me a little shake. "Don't I, *ma petite poule?*"

Amélie and Chloë choked. I gaped at Luc. Mom's eyes narrowed.

Luc smiled at Amélie. "We wanted to keep it *un secret* until we knew we were in love." Luc took Mom's hand and brought it to his lips. "It is *un vrai plaisir* to finally meet the woman who brought my sweet Nadia into the world. Truly, I thank you."

Could he pile it on any thicker? I considered giving him a warning kick on the ankle but Mom was lapping it up. She actually fluttered a hand near her cheek. "My, Nadia, where did you find such a gentleman?"

An hour ago, at a gay bar, *probably* wouldn't cut it as an answer in Mom's world. "Amélie introduced us, actually." It wasn't a lie, but I gave Amélie a look I hoped she'd interpret as "Please shut up." Speaking of introductions, I presented my mom to my friends. "We were all just heading up to my place for a drink."

"We should let you catch up with your mother, Nadia," Chloë said.

"Yes, we wouldn't want to intrude." Amélie edged toward the door to the street. My mother had that effect on people.

"Oh, but Luc should stay!" Apparently Mom was a sucker for hand kisses.

I gave him a graceful out. "He promised to drive Amélie and Chloë home." With any luck, Mom hadn't noticed how tipsy we all were, because no one was going to be driving anyone anywhere.

"Well, then, you'll just have to have him over tomorrow and cook us all dinner. I can't *not* get to know my daughter's new beau while I'm here."

I squirmed. That escalated quickly. "Luc tends to work

late, Mom. I'm not sure he can—"

"*Ne t'en fais pas*, Nadia. I would be honored to dine with you and your mother tomorrow. I will bring the wine." Luc's eyes sparkled with amusement. "7 p.m.?"

"I—" What was I supposed to say? Thanks, fake boyfriend, but no thanks? I decided not to look this gift horse too closely in the mouth. I could swing one dinner and then get Luc to make up a business trip or something, to get him out of Mom's clutches. "7 p.m. sounds great."

Luc grinned. Then he swooped in and planted a wet kiss on my mouth. "*Alors à demain, ma puce.*"

Amélie giggled and they all bustled out the doorway, leaving me staring in stunned confusion after them, my lips still tingling from Luc's kiss.

"Were those girls …?" Mom left the question hanging.

"Yes, Mom, they're a couple."

Mom wrinkled her nose. "That drink sounds divine."

That was the best thing she'd said all night.

CHAPTER THREE

I put the water on medium heat so that it would be on the verge of boiling by the time I needed it to. Mom *knew* I'm a terrible cook, which is why I think she suggested I make dinner in the first place. She's always loved torturing me under the guise of improving my domestic skills.

I'd given her my bed and slept on the couch, then left her to her own devices in the morning after pointing her at the corner café. The internship didn't come with holidays so I couldn't just take the day off at a moment's notice. Amélie had been called away to the Louvre so I'd had no opportunity to quiz her more about Luc.

The more I thought about it now that I'd sobered up, the more uneasy I got about Luc's whole impromptu scheme. We knew nothing about each other. Pretending to be in love with a total stranger? Dinner was going to be a nightmare.

I'd stopped at the *marché* on my way home and picked up some handmade pasta and ingredients for a simple sauce that wouldn't stretch my meager kitchen skills too far.

Luc showed up promptly at seven, bearing the promised wine and a bouquet of flowers. Tonight he wore jeans again, with a tailored, untucked dress shirt in vertical eggplant and black stripes edged with subtle burnt-orange embroidery, over a charcoal T-shirt. The man knew how to dress.

He bussed my cheeks in the typical French greeting and then fawned over Mom again. I gave her a vase and asked her to take care of arranging the flowers, then dragged Luc into my tiny kitchen, where I had the sauce bubbling on the stove.

"What the hell do you think you're doing, Luc?" I said in a low voice.

He set the bottle of wine on the counter, and rummaged in the drawers, presumably for a corkscrew. "I am amusing myself, *chérie*, and helping you at the same time."

"You think this is *funny?*" How was I going to maintain the pretense for a whole evening, much less Mom's whole stay?

"It is hilarious, my dear. But it is also making your mother happy." His accent and insouciant mannerisms made him sound like he was perpetually in on some joke that he *might* share with you, if only you met his standards.

"Look, I appreciate you getting me out of a bind." It *had* been quick, observant thinking on his part. "Let's just have dinner, and then if she asks to sightsee with us or something, just tell her you're going out of town."

"I don't mind showing your *maman* the city. I am between contracts right now, so I am at *liberté.*"

What kind of guy liked to shepherd a stranger's mother

around town? "I don't even know your last name!"

"Du Breuille. *Voilà*, you know everything you need to know."

I threw up my hands, spun around, and planted them on the kitchen island, trying to get a grip on my rising panic. "I don't think this is a good idea," I said, not looking at him.

"*Pourquoi pas?*"

"Because she'll figure it out, and then I'll never hear the end of it. Ever."

Luc came up behind me, set the wine bottle on the counter in front of me, and then wrapped his arm around my other side, trapping me against the island while he busied himself with the corkscrew. His hips grazed my butt, his chest touching my shoulder blades. I stiffened at the complete invasion of my personal space.

"Why would she figure it out?" he breathed softly into my ear, and the whole tenor of the evening changed. His lips brushed the outer edge of my lobe. I became hyperaware of his body against mine. His arm pressed against me as he twisted the corkscrew, his long fingers languidly turning the handle. My heart rate climbed.

"Darling, where do you keep—" Mom stopped her headlong bustle into the kitchen at the tableau before her: the wine bottle, Luc, and me enfolded in his arms, his head against mine, a perfect picture of domestic bliss. "I'm *so* sorry. I didn't mean to intrude." Mom loved to intrude. She must really be impressed with Luc. "I'll be right outside when you're ready with the wine." She backed out into the living room, closing the door behind her.

Luc released the cork and me at the same time, moving to the side to pour three glasses. I stared at him, not quite sure what had just happened. I kept my voice low. I wouldn't put it past my mother to be listening at the door. "Did you just proposition me?"

Luc raised a glass, arched a sardonic eyebrow, and made a toasting motion in my direction. "So perceptive of you. For how long is your mother here?"

"A week."

"If I am to pose as your boyfriend, it is my duty to offer a true simulacrum. Otherwise, where is the fun?"

"But aren't you …"

"Gay?" His lips quirked. "*Non, chérie.* I do not put *limites* on my attractions." His eyes darkened. "And I am *très attiré* to you."

Every hair on my arms stood up.

He picked up another glass of wine. "Think on it, while I bring this to your *maman*. Take your time." Then he sauntered out of the kitchen, leaving me with frissons of disquiet flickering up my spine.

CHAPTER FOUR

I snatched up the remaining wine glass and downed a big swig. Then I stared at the burgundy liquid. Luc *would* have great taste in wine, too.

I wasn't looking for a liaison. I had two months left on this internship. I had reams of work on my plate. Just today, we'd gotten a lead on a missing Manet.

You're in Paris, *Nadia.*

I paced the length of the kitchen, flustered. It *had* been a long time since I'd dumped Ben. That didn't mean I was ready to move on.

I slid my phone out of my pocket. Texted Amélie.

Is Luc good people?

I took another sip of wine.

I'd been willing to entertain the thought of a pretend boyfriend, because

1) I'd panicked, and

2) I'd thought there'd be no strings. Just a small piece of theater to pull the wool over my mother's eyes, get her off my

back.

But this—this was more like method acting. Despite his good looks, I hadn't thought of Luc in any seriously sexual way. Because of where we'd met, and my resulting mistaken assumption. I'd completely misapprehended the situation and his intentions.

A gorgeous Frenchman just said he wanted me.

And he was *very* handsome. Now that my brain had refiled him from "Off Limits" to "Team Nadia," I let my mind's eye rove over his face. Sandy hair, short on the sides, but longer on top, bangs rakishly falling over one eyebrow. Green eyes over high cheekbones in a narrow face, challenging me to take him up on his offer.

I rubbed my arms where his had made contact. The sense memory of his warmth against me invoked in me something I hadn't felt in a long time. Something I'd denied myself.

Desire.

I'd forgotten. It had become easier to forget. Somewhere along the way, between the degree, and Ben, and not wanting to inflict my dysfunctional family on anyone, and maybe even to spite my mother by proving her right about my upcoming spinsterhood, avoiding entanglements turned into the path of least resistance.

When had I turned into this pathetic loner?

You know when, Nadia.

I took another swallow of wine.

My phone buzzed.

THE *BEST*!!!

I typed back.

How far do you trust him?

WITH MY LIFE

I knew his name. He was a snappy dresser, had great taste in wine, an irresistible accent, and Amélie's affection for him spoke volumes. She hadn't steered me wrong about anything in Paris so far.

The only strike against him was that Mom seemed to like him.

I downed the remainder of my glass. Then I grabbed the bottle, poured myself another, and squared my shoulders.

I could handle a little flirting and playacting. I didn't have to take things any further than that. And I *really* didn't want to give Mom an opening to insinuate herself into my love life.

You're in Paris.

Why not?

I pushed through the door into the living room.

CHAPTER FIVE

"You didn't tell me Luc was an *architect!*" Mom primped her perm then placed the hand on his knee. I frowned. It wasn't like her to drink more than a glass of wine, and she'd already had two. It also wasn't like her to get flirty with strange men. I made a mental note to keep an eye on her wine intake, otherwise, against all odds, Luc might have two Fisker women to contend with.

And people wondered why I didn't date.

Luc eyed me over his wine glass, a small smile turning up the left corner of his mouth. "Providing environments for people to realize their full *potentiel* is very—how do you say?—fulfilling. My next project promises to be very exciting."

I refilled his glass and set the bottle on the coffee table. He sprawled casually, one arm on the back of the sofa. He tapped the backrest. *"Tu t'assois?"*

I took the seat next to him. He draped his hand over my shoulder, his knee touching mine. I clinked his glass to avoid thinking about his fingers, which idly caressed my upper arm.

I'd decided I was going to go with this—carpe diem, yadda yadda—but hadn't quite made my peace with it. I took a deep breath. Thought of Luc's question: *Where is the fun?* Trolling my mother might just be the way to go. "To breaking new ground."

Luc's lips quirked. "*Santé.*"

"So you were introduced by your work friend?" Mom asked.

I nodded. Best to stick as close to the real story as possible. "That's right. She'd organized an evening out. Thought it might be fun for me to meet new people."

"How long have I been saying you need to get out more? Look what happens when you do." Mom preened at Luc. "When did you meet?"

Luc looked at me. "It feels like just yesterday, does it not?"

I narrowly avoided snorting wine through my nose. "Time flies when you have chemistry like ours."

Mom sniffed. "Speaking of chemistry, do you smell something burning?"

Oh shit. The sauce. I'd forgotten to turn down the heat. The three of us stood up at the same time. "I've got it, Mom."

"Doesn't smell like it."

"Mom. It's handled." I hurried into the kitchen, where the scent of charred mushrooms and cream told me it decidedly wasn't handled. Fuck. I glanced at the stack of takeout menus next to the fridge. Mom was going to get major "Nadia Never

Learns" mileage out of this one with her bible ladies. My shoulders slumped.

Behind me, the kitchen door hinges squeaked quietly. "Sit, Madame Fisker. Enjoy your wine. I will just check on Nadia." Luc padded up next to me, examining the saucepan with a critical eye. "I presume blackened *je ne sais quoi* was not your intended first course tonight."

I put a despairing hand to my forehead. "I'm so sorry. I ruined dinner."

Luc rubbed the small of my back. "*Mais non.* All is not lost." He picked up the bag of handmade agnolotti from the market I'd left next to the stove. "What is in these?"

"Butternut squash."

"And do you have butter?"

I nodded.

"What about *sauge* … eumh, sage?"

"The mushroom sauce called for sage leaves. I didn't use them all."

"*Merveilleux.* We are set." He took the saucepan off the stove and scraped the wrecked food into the bin. "You should start the pasta. The sauce will only take five minutes."

"Really?"

"*Vraiment.*"

I turned the burner with the pot of simmering water on it to high, then opened the fridge and got out the butter, handing it to Luc. He sliced off several cubes and put them into a fresh frying pan while I retrieved the sage leaves from where I'd stashed them.

We bumped up against each other in the small space, Luc putting his hands on my hips or arms to signal when he wanted to get around me. His touch wasn't lascivious, but lingered sometimes longer than strictly necessary. My skin tingled beneath each place he'd touched like he'd branded me with some sort of electric magic.

The water started to boil as the aroma of melting butter filled the room. Luc dumped the agnolotti into the pot.

"Those are fresh, so they'll only take a few minutes."

"*Parfait.*" The butter now completely melted, Luc tossed several sage leaves into the pan, stirring occasionally.

We sipped our wine in silence, me contemplating my failures in cooking, dating, and meeting parental expectations, Luc studying me while I tried to ignore him.

"It is not *sérieux*, you know. This little *erreur* is easily fixed."

"Sure. But it's also another item in Mom's ongoing 'Nadia Fails at *Real* Womanhood' list."

Luc gave me an appraising look. "You look like a *real* woman to me."

I deflected that comment by grabbing the pot of pasta and upending it into the colander in the sink. "Is that ready? I'm just not sure how a little butter and sage is going to rescue dinner." I was feeling sorry for myself, even if it did smell delicious.

"Give it here."

I passed him the colander, and he poured the agnolotti into the pan. The butter sizzled, a bit like my skin where Luc touched me. The fat had turned a warm brown, the sage crispy and aromatic. He stirred the pasta around, coating each little pouch with sauce, and turned off the heat.

Then he dragged a finger along the bowl of his stirring spoon, and held it up to me. "*Goûte*." When I eyed him sceptically, he waggled the finger a little. "Go ahead. Taste."

I leaned forward, parted my lips, and licked his finger tentatively. The flavor burst across my tongue, nutty and earthy and rich. "Mmmmhh, that's good."

"Is it? I must try." But instead of using his spoon or licking his finger, Luc cupped my nape, leaned down, and kissed me, his tongue teasing at my still parted lips. Then he let me go. "*Oui*. But it needs some pepper." He grabbed the mill I kept next to the stove and ground some out.

I just stood there like a dumbstruck teenager until he glanced at me from beneath an arched eyebrow, that annoying, knowing smile just tilting the corner of his mouth. "Do you have plates? This will get cold."

I shook myself out of my stupor and grabbed the dishes from the cupboard.

Luc divvied up the pasta between the bowls, finishing with a flourish. "*Et voilà!* What did I tell you? No *problème* at all."

Steam wafted up from the plates as he hefted two and bumped open the kitchen door with his hip. I grabbed the remaining dish.

I might have kissed him again if I wasn't feeling like such a self-conscious fool.

CHAPTER SIX

Mom put both hands to her cheeks. "Oh my! That smells delightful."

"I assure you, it is, Madame Fisker." Luc set down a dish at the head of the table and offered Mom a seat. He took his own plate and sat to her left. I took the seat facing him, to her right.

"Thank you for saving my daughter from herself."

I gritted my teeth.

"But I cannot take credit for this, Madame Fisker. It was all Nadia."

I widened my eyes at him in warning. There was believable, and then there was me in a kitchen. But Mom didn't notice—she was too engrossed in his accent. "I'm sure you helped."

Luc gave me a sly smile. "I performed the taste test, yes."

I pushed back my chair and got up. This was going to call for more wine. "Dig in. I'll be right back."

I retrieved a bottle from my emergency stash in the

kitchen and hurriedly uncorked it. When I returned, Mom was a quarter of the way through her plate but Luc was still patiently waiting for me. I refilled the glasses, sat down, and picked up my fork.

Luc raised his glass. "To unforeseen pleasures."

Mom looked a little puzzled at that one but clinked his glass. Luc ignored her, his eyes fastened to mine.

I inclined my glass to his. Took a sip as he did as well, never dropping my gaze. Some mutual understanding passed between us, and a little lock inside me snicked open. Game on. A little flirting couldn't hurt now, could it? Besides, this whole ruse needed propping up if I didn't want Mom to sniff me out.

"Mom, is there anything in particular you want to see while you're here?"

I took a bite of agnolotti and closed my eyes with pleasure as Mom rambled on about museums and arrondissements and the Eiffel Tower. The butter, sage, and squash dissolved on my tongue. This was quite possibly the best simple meal I'd ever had. I let out a deep, satisfied breath. When I opened my eyes again, Luc winked at me. I brought my fork to my mouth and slowly popped another bite in, closing my lips softly over the tines and easing the fork out, taking my time, savoring both the flavors and the increasing intensity in Luc's eyes.

I turned my attention back to Mom. "If you haven't been to the Louvre, that's always worth a stop, but my personal favorite is the Musée de l'Orangerie." I had never realized just how big Monet's *Nymphéas* were, and the emotional punch of their full-size splendor had nearly brought me to tears. I'd sat in that room for hours, just basking in the beauty.

"Oh, flowers and ponds. Yawn. I get enough of those back in Vancouver. I think I'll do a *bateau-mouche* tour instead. Can you not get even one day off to show me around?"

Showing my mother the "sights" usually meant lots of shopping. And I was an indifferent shopper at best. "Maybe if you'd given me some notice, Mom. You'll still be here on Saturday. I'll get you a pass for the Métro and you'll be just fine until then. I can show you around in the evenings after work."

The main course done, I brought out a cheese plate.

Mom spread some brie on her cracker. "So tell me about your first date."

"It was *formidable*."

I nodded. "You took me to that little place … what was it called?"

"Le Feu au Lac. You remember, we had that wonderful *saumon à la provençale*."

I winced.

Mom's eyes widened. "But Nadia's allergic to salmon."

Luc didn't skip a beat. "And that is when I knew I wanted to see more of her. Holding her hand at *l'hôpital*, I saw how brave she is … you have quite the daughter, Madame Fisker."

Mom sat in stunned silence, eyes tracking from Luc to me and back again. "But, Nadia, you *know* you're allergic to salmon."

"He's just pulling your leg, Mom. *Luc* had the salmon. I had the *moules frites.*"

Luc slapped the table. "*Mais oui.* I had forgotten. That explains our first kiss. Mussels are an aphrodisiac."

Mom pursed her lips. "I should hope things have gone no further than that."

I sighed. "You needn't have any worries in that department, Mom."

Luc looked puzzled. "You disapprove of sex, Madame Fisker?"

"Outside of marriage, yes."

"But that is the best kind." Luc sat back, nonplussed.

"Not where my daughter is concerned."

"Mom, the French have very different attitudes regarding love." I gave Luc a slight warning shake of the head.

"We didn't raise you to adopt foreign mores at the drop of a hat, Nadia."

"If it was only a question of how you raised me, I'd still be a virgin. But I haven't been for a while"—Luc grinned —"so why don't we drop the topic of sex and talk about tomorrow. I might be able to leave work a little early and walk you around town a bit."

"If you are not sick of me already, Madame Fisker, I could meet you both for dinner. I know a great little restaurant near the Canal St-Martin."

I gave Luc my most unobtrusive "what are you doing?" look. "I thought you had a business trip this week."

"I leave next week, *ma chouette.*"

Flirting for one night might be one thing, but now we were practically going on a second date. "I don't know … Mom's only here for a few days."

"Far be it from me to part you two lovebirds." I guess Mom had decided to overlook our potential transgressions. "Besides, Aunt Liz will be so jealous when I tell her I got squired around Paris by a real Frenchman."

Luc stood up. "Then it is *tout réglé*. Dinner tomorrow." He looked at me. "It is late, and I think your mother is tired."

I nodded. "I'll see you out."

Luc shrugged on his jacket, and I followed him into the hall, shutting the door behind me. Turning, I said, "You really don't need to—" I bumped straight into Luc's chest.

"Oh, but I do." His hand slid up my back as he bent down and covered my mouth with his.

"Mmph." I pressed my hands to the leather of his jacket, breathing in the scent of his skin mingled with red wine and a hint of sage. There was no one here to see us, no one to playact for. But he smelled so good, his lips soft against mine, gentle and playful. My hands slid of their own volition up to frame his throat, his stubble pricking the tips of my fingers.

The elevator ground up to my floor and I pulled away. Luc smiled down at me. "I will convince you yet, *mon poussin*. Meet me at the corner of Rue des Récollets and Quai de Valmy at 7:30 p.m."

I didn't *want* to be convinced. Staying stubbornly single meant zero possibility of betrayal. But the memory of Luc's lips against mine, his arms around me, the desire in his eyes for me—*me*, not some other objective—evoked sensations in my chest I'd long suppressed.

And I did want to keep Mom from any thoughts of further matchmaking. That was the real goal here. *Keep your eyes on the prize, Nadia.* It certainly didn't hurt that Luc was so easy on those eyes. Maybe a little too easy.

"Your mother, she is a bit of a prude, *non?*"

"You don't know the half of it."

"Is it a case of 'like mother, like daughter?' "

"I am nothing like my mother."

Luc leaned in, I thought for a quick buss goodbye. But his lips played against my cheek and he breathed softly into my ear. "Good. There is hope for us yet." He caressed my lower lip with his thumb, and I found myself stretching forward to follow his touch as he backed slowly into the elevator. He was reawakening sensations and wants I'd determinedly packed away. "*À demain, ma belle.*"

"I … look forward to it."

As I reentered my apartment, I tried to assure myself that I was just being polite.

I failed.

CHAPTER SEVEN

IN the cold light of day, I cursed myself for not nipping this whole wacky plan in the bud from the beginning. Why was Luc so impossible to say no to? I'd jumped out of the frying pan and into the fire. The irony that none of this would have happened but for Mom didn't escape me either, which led inevitably to thoughts of Ben.

I'd had a string of bad luck involving men with ulterior motives. There was Eric, who dumped me as soon as he learned my PhD supervisor would not be evaluating his dissertation. And before that, Vlad, who it turned out was looking for someone to marry after the government denied his permanent residency. Jae had just really wanted into my roommate's pants, and Ahmad a place outside his parents' home to store his drugs—he was *really* unhappy when he found out I'd flushed them, but I drew a solid line at narcotics.

But Ben—Ben had taken the proverbial cake and smashed it on the floor, smearing the icing all over the cracked tiles of my heart.

Ben had walked in to the gallery I was clerking at to supplement my tuition, asked me some really beginner questions about the paintings on the wall, then invited me out for coffee. I'd seen him around campus, and he seemed nice, if a little shy and straight-laced, with blond, boy-next-door good looks. He was studying theology, which led to some interesting conversations given my abandonment of the faith I'd been brought up in. Coffee became dinner and a movie, and before long too long I'd taken a serious fall for him.

For the first time in years, my parents didn't give me disappointed looks when I introduced a boyfriend to them. They hadn't warmed to many of the men I'd brought home during what Mom still referred to as my "rebellious phase"— a phase I'd never managed to convince her I'd never grow out of. They had fond hopes of bringing me back into the parish fold. While I steadfastly refused to satisfy them on that front, it felt good to finally have someone they approved of in my life, who didn't draw sceptical looks or outright recrimination —someone who might actually stand a chance of fitting in the prim little boxes they expected me to live in.

Ben was sweet, and considerate, but pretty soon it became apparent that we had very differing views on sex before marriage. My parents were over the moon that he was "saving" himself, but I was a little less enthused to leave things at heavy petting. I'd abandoned a lot of beliefs when I left the church, much to the benefit of my sex life, and this felt like a step backwards to me.

"It's not wrong if we love each other," I told Ben one night in front of the TV. I'd been nuzzling his neck, and he'd carefully pushed aside my roving hand.

"If we love each other, it'll be that much better if we wait."

"And if we're not physically compatible?" I slipped my hand between the buttons of his shirt, stroked his chest. He clasped my wrist and brought my knuckles to his lips.

"If we're compatible in every other way, that shouldn't matter."

"Shouldn't it?"

"You're my best friend, Nadia. One day you'll be my lover too, and we'll be great together. Just not tonight."

Given all his other great qualities, I figured why not wait a little. I'd sown my own wild oats in the past, and wasn't in any particular hurry. If he wasn't bothered that I was no longer a virgin, maybe I should cut him some slack about wanting to stay one. Besides, I didn't have to live my *entire* life in direct opposition to my parents' beliefs. That couldn't be healthy.

And it was true. Ben and I *were* best friends. We talked and told each other everything about our hopes and dreams —or so I'd thought. I opened up to him about the constant sea of guilt I swam in by keeping my parents at a distance, something I felt I had to do to preserve my own sanity and sense of self after I broke with them over the faith I'd grown up in.

Ben made me feel loved and listened to, and I began to think he might be the person I'd like to spend the rest of my life with. Someone who could even bridge the gap with my family.

After we'd been dating for six months, I asked him to move in with me. Instead he pulled out an engagement ring. I opened my mouth to say yes, then the thought of the PhD I had to finish intruded. But that's what long engagements were for, weren't they?

He misinterpreted the hesitation on my face. "It'll be fine, Nadia. You'll see. After your dad's given me the ministry—"

An alarm bell clanged in my head. "What do you mean 'given you the ministry?' "

Ben paled, stammered. "I—it's just … your parents said that after we were married, I could come on board, and eventually—"

"When?" Cold fingers of suspicious rage crawled up my spine.

"In a few years of course. After I've learned about the parish. Our future's assured."

"No. When did they make you this offer?" Ben had been to dinner with my parents exactly once, and I didn't remember any opportunities for sidebar discussions on that occasion. Mostly because I nipped most of those in the bud in the interest of keeping my parents' noses out of my private business.

"I—"

"When, Ben?"

"Last Christmas."

Nine months prior. Before I'd even met him.

I put the ring back in Ben's hand, walked to the door of my apartment, and held it open. "Get out."

"Nadia, it's not what you think."

"So you didn't agree to date me—to *marry* me—to satisfy your own ambition?"

"It's not like that. I would never have done it if I didn't think we could make a life together. I wasn't sure at first, but I do love you."

"Get. Out." I couldn't even look at him anymore, and I feared I might say worse.

When I'd confronted my parents, I'd discovered Ben was the son of a fellow minister my father knew from his own seminary days. The lot of them had sold me off to a nice young man who embodied all the qualities my parents despaired of in me, in the hopes that I would rejoin the faith.

I'd thought that despite the lack of sex, Ben and I were intimate. But it had all been a lie built on a foundation of disrespect for my own desires. He'd kept the most important parts of himself hidden from me behind a mask of moral rectitude.

I'd sworn off men since—because I had no idea what it would take to get me to trust one again.

And here was Luc—charming, clearly attracted to me, and with no possible ties to my screwed-up family. His touch reminded me of all the things I'd denied myself since dumping Ben—hell, *while* dating Ben even. My heart wanted to avoid messy entanglements, but I'd be lying to myself if I didn't admit that my body wanted nothing more than to tangle my limbs with Luc's.

Luc had made it seem like this was all just a game to him, but most games had a goal, and I couldn't figure out his.

Some games are just played for fun.

Was it really that simple? The part of me that had been toyed with too many times refused to believe it.

Yet here I stood anyway, by a bench on the Canal St-Martin, waiting for Luc to meet me and Mom for dinner. He was fifteen minutes late already. If he stood me up, all my problems might be solved.

"Why don't you text him?" Mom plopped her plumpish frame down on the bench and reached down to massage the tops of her feet through her sensible pumps.

It was a great suggestion. But stupid me hadn't gotten his phone number when he came over last night.

I tried to distract her with questions of my own. "What did you think of Le Marais?"

We'd spent the last hour walking through the trendy neighborhood, filled with chic little boutiques and artist ateliers. We'd started near the Seine at the Village St-Paul, where I'd taken her antiquing, then meandered along the cobbles of Rue des Barres, past its medieval timbered *maisons à colombages* and the crowds spending a lazy evening at the many outdoor patios.

As we'd made our way northward to meet Luc, I'd even managed to find the secret nook Amélie had shown me when I'd first arrived, the Passage de l'Ancre, a hidden little alleyway lined with colorful offices and potted plants, a quiet oasis amid the bustle of the city.

"It felt a little bohemian for my taste."

I rolled my eyes. Count on Mom to find something to criticize for any occasion. My foot twitched impatiently. Where was Luc?

"Does he live near here? Maybe we could knock on his door, see what's holding him up."

"I don't know …" Crap. I had no clue which arrondissement Luc lived in, much less his street, but couldn't let Mom get a whiff of my ignorance. "… that that's the greatest idea, Mom. He could be on a client call and I wouldn't want to interrupt."

"Seriously, Nadia, just text him."

I wasn't about to admit I couldn't do that, but I whipped out my phone anyway. I could text Amélie and she could pass along his number. Before I could hit "Send", Luc strode around the corner.

"*Mes excuses*, my meeting ran late."

"I thought you were between projects," Mom said.

"That does not mean I do not have other potential clients to talk to. Come, the restaurant is this way."

He led us a block away from the canal to a typical small Parisian French restaurant, a tiny hole-in-the-wall with warm wood paneling and a mosaic-tiled ceiling. We had our choice of tables, dining early compared to most Parisians to accommodate Mom's jet lag.

I ordered perch meunière, Mom chose the roasted chicken with potatoes au gratin, and Luc a beef filet. As we waited for the food to arrive, Luc reached out and took my hand in his, thumb caressing my knuckles, fingers tickling my palm. If I jerked away, I'd blow the whole image of two people who'd been dating for weeks now right out of the water, so I just sat there and let him have his way with my hand.

Luc's eyes twinkled in amusement as he felt the tension in my wrist. He had me right where he wanted me.

If I was being honest with myself, I wasn't sure *I* wasn't right where I wanted to be. Luc had the sensuous hands of an artist, and the soft tracery of his fingers against my palm raised goosebumps up my arm. Because of course my mind decided it had nothing better to contemplate than what sensations those fingers might draw out elsewhere on my skin.

Luc's smile deepened as a flush spread across my cheeks, which forced me to bat aside further thoughts of what artistry his lips might be capable of. I shifted slightly in my chair at the sudden tension in my groin.

"So how serious are you two, anyway?" Count on Mom to provide a distraction.

"About as serious as most couples who've known each other as long as we have." I was getting good at not actually lying.

"Your father and I were really hoping to see you settled by now."

And they'd done their underhanded best to see to it. "It's a little early to be talking marriage, Mom."

"But not, perhaps, too early to discuss living in sin, *non?*" Luc arched a sardonic eyebrow, and I got the sudden impression that the game of teasing Fisker women now involved more victims.

"Your apartment *is* lovely." I took a sip of wine. Mom's eyebrows climbed into her hairline. There was a lot to be said for this game. "But I suspect it's a little soon."

"How does the English expression go? 'Resistance is futile?' "

"On the contrary. *'Vive la résistance.'* "

But more and more, I felt my resolve slipping. Every time he touched me, Luc simply made me feel too good. And it didn't hurt at all that he'd managed to thoroughly flummox Mom. The days when I chose a man to please my parents were never coming back. *That*, at least, was a vow I could stick to.

Our food arrived, allowing me to retrieve my hand from Luc's, and giving Mom some time to figure out her next salvo. She'd pursed her lips at Luc's proposition. Maybe the bloom was coming off the French rose for her. Which couldn't help but increase his allure for me.

Dinner mostly proceeded amid the clink of cutlery and the calm of quiet conversation, until Mom decided to get nosy again. "Are you a man of faith, Luc?"

"I have faith in humanity. That is enough for me."

"But surely—"

"How's your chicken, Mom?" Religion was a topic better steered clear of, even if Luc could probably hold his own.

But she ignored the hint. "Nadia, I'm perfectly within my rights to get to know your friend here better. I just want what's best for you."

"I suspect I'm the better judge of what's best for me."

"I should think that past history might have disabused you of that idea."

A muscle jumped in my jaw from the effort of not spitting out my first bitter retort. Not here. Not in front of Luc. I took a deep breath. "I—"

Luc reached out and stroked my cheek. He spoke to my mother. "The past is *fini.*" Then he fixed his gaze to mine. "I am only interested in the future, *mon trésor.* Can you not see it as well? The one I see is beautiful."

I stared at him, suddenly lost in his green eyes, eyes filled with warmth and empathy. And desire.

For a fake boyfriend, he was doing admirably well at making me feel cherished.

My mother's endless critiques, of my single status, then the men I brought home—not to mention the whole thing with Ben—had acted like dating aversion therapy, to the point where I'd lost sight of how good being *seen* could feel.

I thought Ben had seen me, but I only represented the fulfillment of his ambitions. Luc had known me two days and based on the way he expertly deflected my mother's sniping microaggressions, already seemed to understand so much without me having to explain a single thing. I gave Luc a slow smile of my own, to let him know that finally, I saw him too.

Maybe his motives didn't matter. Maybe the only thing

that mattered was allowing in a little joy.

The waiter brought the dessert menu. Going with my newfound epiphany, I ordered the chocolate lava cake. When it arrived ten minutes later, Mom stood up. "Is the little girls' room at the back?"

Luc pointed it out and she wandered off.

I contemplated the cake for a moment. Embracing a dessert was a whole lot easier than letting go of my compulsive distrust. Aside from weight gain, the cake couldn't hurt me. *Fuck it, Nadia, just* ask *him.* "Luc, what exactly are you hoping to get out of our little arrangement?"

"Is the presence of a beautiful, intelligent woman in my life, and perhaps my bed, not enough?"

"Is it?" I wanted to believe him so badly.

"I am not a complicated man, Nadia."

I dug into my cake, which fulfilled all of its advertised gooey promise. What if I just took Luc at his word too?

Luc eyed the molten chocolate oozing onto the plate. "May I?"

I nodded, my own mouth too occupied with chocolatey goodness.

Luc reached out and coated his fingertip with chocolate. Instead of tasting it, though, he swept the finger down the side of my throat. "*Ah, zut. Quel dégât.*" But he didn't sound disappointed at all. He leaned over, and licked the chocolate from my neck, putting the still chocolate-coated finger to my lips.

I could have refused. Could have leaned away. Could have

called the whole thing off right there, given in to my inner voice of doubt, said thank you and goodnight, collected my mother, and gone home.

Instead, I closed my eyes and leaned into his lips—soft and warm against the hollow behind my jaw—drew his finger into my mouth, and gently sucked away the chocolate. I let out the tiniest sigh, savoring the rich sweetness mingled with Luc's scent, his touch and closeness. Then I remembered where I was and sat back, worried I'd made a spectacle of myself. But no one seemed to have observed—or if they had, they were being very discreet about it.

I almost didn't notice Mom's return, I was so focused on returning Luc's intense stare. "Was your dessert not any good?" Mom eyed the half-destroyed cake in front of me.

I didn't take my eyes from Luc's. "Best dessert ever."

Luc's lips twitched.

"But you didn't finish it."

"It was too much for me." I set my fork down onto the plate. "I surrender."

Luc pushed back his chair. "I am sorry to eat and run, but I double-booked myself tonight. You remember, it's Marjolaine's birthday *soirée*. She will be disappointed—she was looking forward to meeting you."

"Oh, right. It's been so busy, I forgot. You'll give her my regrets?" I adlibbed.

"I didn't mean to sideline your plans," Mom said.

"It's not to worry, the party will go late, and this was important." Luc bussed my mother's cheek.

"If you were invited too, Nadia, shouldn't you go?" Mom asked.

"Marjolaine is a colleague, and I'm sure she'll understand. But Nadia is always *la bienvenue*."

"Oh, I'm still jetlagged and was just about to fall into bed anyway. You kids go have fun."

I gave Luc an uncertain look. It wasn't like me to just crash—or rather have my mother encourage me to crash—someone else's party. And Mom *had* come all the way here to see me. She might claim she was fine now but she would probably give me hurt looks in the morning. "That's OK, Mom—"

"I will not keep Nadia very late, I promise." Luc shrugged on his leather jacket, then held mine up for me to slide into.

"Are you sure this is fine?" I muttered to him.

"*Oui, bien sûr.*"

"We'll walk you to the Métro, Mom." We weren't very far from La Gare de l'Est train station, where three different subway lines also intersected. I grabbed my purse and dealt with the bill, then met Luc and Mom on the sidewalk outside. We dropped her off at the right platform.

As her train pulled away, I turned to Luc. "So where is this party?"

Luc's eyes glittered like dark emeralds. He took my hand and led me towards a different platform. "There is no party."

CHAPTER EIGHT

"WHAT you need right now is *not* more time with that woman. Now that we have satisfied your mother, it is time we satisfied ourselves. What do you say?"

The platform grew narrower as we locked our gazes, neither one of us wanting to look away.

Why should I deny myself pleasure out of fears rooted in the past? I had nothing to offer Luc except myself, which he'd made abundantly plain he wanted.

I'd tried to please my parents and look where that had gotten me. Why should I feel any guilt about wanting to please myself?

Finally, I cleared my throat. "Just so I'm clear about this, you're bi, right?"

Luc nodded. "Does that trouble you?"

I took my time answering as we navigated the tunnel to our platform. When I'd been a naïve teenager steeped in the orthodoxy of my family's evangelical faith, my knee-jerk answer would have been yes. But various friends and fellow students had gradually opened my eyes to how close-minded, and even harmful, those attitudes were, and I'd … changed. Much to my parents' ceaseless chagrin, but that, I could live with.

The question had never come up with any of my own previous partners though, which isn't to say that none of them might have been bisexual. But even if whatever this thing Luc had started was built on a lie for my mother, if we were to actually take this further, we needed to be open with each other. I'd experienced too much grief because of people keeping things from me.

So he'd slept with women before me. And men.

I'd slept with my fair share of men. Was it any different?

"I don't think so?" I couldn't help the slight question in my voice. "I've just never had a bi partner before."

"As far as you know." He wedged my arm in the crook of his elbow and we walked to our train.

"Where are you taking me?"

"Where I can have my way with you." He arched an enquiring eyebrow at me. "If that meets with your approval."

The sudden warm tension low in my belly told me I most definitely approved. "It does."

"*Formidable.*" He lifted my arm and brushed his lips along my knuckles. The back of my neck tingled as I imagined his lips elsewhere. "It is not far." His tongue slid between my fingers, soft and warm in the webbing between, then he turned my hand over and kissed my palm deeply. "Just far enough for me to plant pictures in your head of what is to come."

I inhaled as he smiled his slow, knowing smile at me.

We picked up the pace, finally arrived at our platform. I fidgeted during the interminable wait for the train. There were no seats on the one that finally pulled in, so I gripped the central pole. Luc stood just behind me, his body pressed against mine in the car filled with soccer fans returning from a match. He leaned down and nuzzled my ear. "When was the last time someone made love to you?" No one else could hear him over the noise of the train.

"It's … been a while."

He tutted softly. "You need to take better care of yourself, *ma belle*."

I leaned back against him. He wasn't wrong. The train jerked and he wrapped an arm around my waist, his forearm braced against my stomach. My butt pressed against his thighs, his hard warmth.

The hand at my waist slipped behind my jacket, beneath my shirt, his palm caressing my flank. His fingers snuck below the waistband of my jeans and stroked my hip. "*Dis-moi*, do you like it, having someone fuck you?" My breath caught.

At the other end of the car, a group of football fans started chanting raucous slogans. A woman seated in front of us glanced as us then quickly away. I didn't think she could see Luc's hand, but for once I forgot to concern myself with what others might think of our PDA.

Luc's voice hummed low in my ear, insidious, sowing the

seeds he'd promised. "Because that is what I am going to do. I will set your skin afire with my mouth. I will tease until you beg me to stop. Until you beg me not to. We are going to have such fun together, *ma mignonne*. You will see."

My lips had parted and I squeezed his wrist. The train pulled into the next station. "Are we there yet?" I husked. Now that I'd given in, my impatience flared like the heat seething through my body.

"One more stop."

The doors opened and the woman got up, looking less than impressed with us as she exited the train. The footballers continued their bawdy singing.

Luc smiled against my ear. He spent the short minutes until the next station murmuring increasingly filthy promises. I closed my eyes and ground ever so slightly against his hips. "*Patience, chérie.* We are almost there."

The train screeched into the station. The doors opened, and just like that, Luc's arm released me, the sudden loss of his warmth and presence like being ejected from a sauna. We practically jogged up the stairs to the street, but that wasn't why I was panting.

CHAPTER NINE

His flat was two blocks from the station, a third-floor walkup. Stark white walls, high ceilings, weathered wood beams, and wide-plank wood floors created a modern rustic vibe, which he'd amped up with rough-hewn wooden antiques mixed with more spartan contemporary pieces, and a plush, white slip-covered sofa with piles of cushions. Black-framed artwork hung from the walls or lay propped on mantels and sideboards. A door to the left opened to an office with casual clutter, several scale mockups of buildings lying on the floor and the desk.

Luc came behind me, deftly sweeping my jacket from my shoulders as I shrugged it off. He draped it over a chair next to the sideboard, held my hair aside, and played his lips across the nape of my neck. I shivered.

"Such an elegant neck. Would you like a digestif?" He trailed his fingers from my shoulder down along my arm, then down my thigh, before coming back up to fondle the curve of my ass.

I shook my head. Why would he want to slow things down now?

"Very well. I would be remiss as a host had I not asked." His voice dripped liquid lust into my brain. It didn't matter what he said anymore, it all sounded sexy in that slightly amused accent of his.

He took a step forward, his thigh between my legs, his weight unbalancing me, forcing me ahead as well. I took the hint and we stumbled, partially entwined, to the couch, his lips hot at my ear the whole time, his tongue licking my lobe. He spun us slightly and we sank down onto the cushions.

My mouth found his and, greedy with delayed gratification, I feasted on his lips and tongue. His mouth was lush, warm, soft, and open to me, and he greeted my tongue with enthusiasm and a low noise in the back of his throat. His hand drifted up my back beneath my shirt, clasping me close, caressing my spine, while the other cradled my head, his fingers mussing my hair. I scrubbed my palm along the back of his scalp against the grain, reveling in the rough nap of the bristles of his hair against my skin.

For endless minutes we learned the taste of each other. I lost myself in the pleasure of his touch, in the give and take of our mouths, of his hungry lips. All pretense fled, burned away by a clean, honest physicality. I clutched him to me, my breasts flattened against his chest, as his long hands stroked my shoulders and my flank, slid beneath my jeans and flattened against my cheeks, both of us craving the heat of the other's body.

His fingers deftly released the clasp of my bra, and he broke the kiss only to raise my shirt over my head, taking the bra with it. I pressed my chest against his, the cotton of his shirt grazing my nipples. Then I shifted, straddled him, and busied my own fingers at the buttons of his shirt, sliding it from his shoulders and slipping my hands beneath the T-shirt underneath. Beneath me, his cock pulsed once, and my loins answered.

My hands glided up, tracing the outline of his torso and the contours of his hard abs, drawing the T-shirt with them. I circled my thumbs over his nipples as I went higher, and he inhaled sharply, the nubs going erect as my thumbs did slow, lazy rounds. Then I let my hands continue, up, across his pits and along his tautly muscled triceps as he raised his arms and helped tug the shirt over his head.

We both paused then, me with both palms on his chest. He had a swimmer's build, sculpted biceps flowing into broad shoulders, a deep chest narrowing down to a trim waist. He stared up at me and swept a hand along my brow and cheek, trailing my hair through his fingers, framing my shoulder before coming back up to cup the line of my jaw.

The dark glimmer in his eyes still conveyed overtones of playful amusement, but now it was overlaid with something else. "You are a lovely *surprise, chaton.* I did not expect you to accept my offer."

"No one is more surprised than I am." But I softened that by kissing his forehead.

He leaned in and kissed my throat, working his way up

along the hollow beneath my jaw. "*J'adore les surprises.*"

I tilted my head back, closed my eyes, and let him explore my neck and shoulders, his mouth eager against my skin, tongue drawing warm trails in its wake. One hand supported my back, while the other came round to cup my breast. His thumb flicked across my nipple, back and forth, gentle as a paintbrush. I drew in a deep breath, my chest straining for more of his touch. My world ended where his started, the boundaries of our skin creating points of union. His mouth never left me as he dipped his head and licked around my other aureola, then took my nipple between his lips. He sucked slowly, taking long, deep pulls, his tongue whorling, shooting stabs of pleasure straight down to my groin.

I rocked my hips against his, the bulge of his cock hard against me.

He chuckled, his hot breath warm on my breast. "Not yet, *chaton*. I warned you I'm a tease." Then he turned his attention to the other breast, suckling strongly, lingering at the end of each pull to circle his tongue around my now rock hard peak. I moaned quietly, ground down into his hips again. He buried his head in my chest, pulling me against him, his stubble scraping my skin as he divided his attentions between both sides, mouth clamped to me, hand kneading and stroking. I rubbed my groin against his, undulating in time with his pulls. He groaned and slid the hand on my back down, inside my jeans, his fingers squeezing my ass, brushing the edge of my cleft, reaching low to cup the place where my thigh met my cheek.

I wanted out of these jeans so badly, wanted to rid myself of all barriers between us. He might be a tease, but he knew what he was about. Hesitant before, I was all in now. He'd fired up every single one of my nerve endings, and if he had eight hands and three mouths I still wouldn't be able to get enough. I wanted him to wrap himself around me, let myself sink into his embrace, have his desire and mine blend and merge until neither of us knew where one of us started and the other left off.

As if reading my mind, he shifted out from under me, twisted, and laid me down against the cushions. He reached into what I'd taken for a decorative pot on the end table, and retrieved a foil wrapper. Then he knelt between my legs and unbuttoned his fly. He slid his jeans and briefs down his hips, releasing his cock. I bit my lower lip, transfixed by his glistening tip.

"You like?"

I nodded.

He was uncircumcised. I reached out a tentative finger to touch his foreskin. He grabbed my hand and placed it on his shaft, closing his fingers around mine. His girth filled my palm perfectly. Together we rubbed up and down along his whole length. He groaned softly and pumped his hips forward, once, and again.

He released my hand and pushed my arm away, then opened the condom wrapper and sheathed himself, adjusting his foreskin back in place. Then he reached for the button of my own jeans, unzipped the fly, and eased them down my hips, pulling backwards until my legs were free. After dropping my pants on the floor, he finished removing his own.

He knelt once again between my knees, his hands stroking up my thighs, moving all the way to my belly, around my hips then just beneath my ass, back down my hamstrings to my knees, then up the inside with an insistent pressure that made me spread my legs more. He stopped then at the crease where my thighs met my hips, and I tilted my pelvis to greet his palms.

I watched him watching me, his expression intent, taking in my every reaction to his touch. He smiled that crooked smile of his.

He spread his thumbs wide, sending them deep into the folds of my labia. I closed my eyes and lost myself in his touch. He massaged my crevices, slicking me, his thumbs moving in opposing circles. One found my clit, and I arched my back, while the other made a slow circuit of the edge of my hole.

He bent down, kissed my navel, exhaled onto my mound, slid his body further down the couch between my legs, his thumbs relentless in their lazy exploration of my cunt.

My breath came ever faster while he toyed with me. I opened my eyes, tilted my head up to look down at him. His chin was resting just above my slit, mouth to my pubis, his hot breath dewing my skin. He returned my gaze, never altering the rhythm of his thumbs. I writhed beneath him, reached out, pressed gently against the top of his head.

"Are you sure the time is right, *chaton?*"

I growled at him.

He grinned. "Very well." Then he plunged his head between my legs and licked the entire length of my slit, down and then up again. "*Quel délice,*" he murmured, before clamping his mouth to my clit and taking a long, slow draw.

I moaned and pushed my hips against his face. The muscles of my vaginal wall tightened and my clit pulsed beneath his tongue. The nerves at the base of my spine sent pleasure signals radiating throughout my entire body.

He sucked languidly, the same way he'd done at my breasts, taking seconds at a time, his tongue doing the round of my nub and his lips encouraging it to leave the protection of its hood. He kept a leisurely tempo that drove me increasingly wild. I'd explode if he didn't give me release soon. I undulated my hips and arched, urging him on, but he maintained his maddeningly deliberate pace.

"Luc." I writhed, at my wits end, squeezed my eyes shut. "Uunh. Luc!" My voice cracked. "*Lu-uc!*"

The soft wetness of his mouth vanished without warning. My eyes flew open at this outrage, to find him propping himself above me. He grasped his cock and entered me with one measured thrust. I took him in, reveling in the feel of him filling me. He fit me like a missing puzzle piece. He thrust once, twice, short and hard, fingered my clit and thrust again, and I came so suddenly I yelped. My thighs spasmed and I clutched at the sheets as my orgasm overtook me.

Luc loomed over me, taking in my pleasure. He rocked

his hips back and thrust into me again, his hands kneading my breasts. I pumped my hips against his as we established a new beat, faster, more up-tempo. This time I watched his face, his focus as he penetrated me deeply, my gaze never leaving his. His hand came up to my face, caressed my cheek, his thumb brushing my lips.

As he drove in to his deepest point, I clenched the muscles of my inner walls, clamping down on his shaft. Luc grunted, threw his head back, and spasmed within me, bucking against my pelvis as I bore down against him to receive the entire measure of his release.

He sank back, his cock still pulsing inside me. "That was not entirely fair, *chérie.*"

"Payback's a bitch." I basked in the warm glow of mutual repletion.

Luc slid out from me, leaned forward, and smoothed the hair from my damp forehead. "You are exquisite *en ce moment.*"

"I bet you say that to all your lovers."

"I do." There was not a drop of mockery in his gaze. "Because it's true. You are all beautiful in these moments. The looks you give me from beneath hooded eyes, your skin flushed and glistening with sweat, your hair in disarray. I love you like this, love bringing you all to this, making you, as we say in French, *rassasiée* … sated."

It was my turn to give him a mischievous look. "Would that that were true."

Luc snorted softly. "*C'est comme ça, einh?* That will not do. Not at all."

CHAPTER TEN

Luc extricated himself from between my legs and sat on the edge of the couch.

He pushed against my hip, rocking me slightly. "Roll over. *Alors vas-y*, on your stomach." His tone brooked no nonsense. I wondered if I was about to regret my challenge.

But I turned over, clutching one of the sofa pillows to my chest to prop my head and torso up a bit. Luc skimmed his hand over my calf, up past my knee, along my hamstring, pausing in his upward trajectory to rub my bottom, spreading his fingers and massaging lightly.

"Such a lovely ass," he murmured. "Here, we call it *callipyge*." His thumb insinuated itself between my cheeks and the pad brushed lightly against my most private hole.

I gasped in shock and stiffened.

"Has no one ever touched you there before?"

"Never."

"It will be our little secret then." He pressed ever so gently but didn't penetrate me. It didn't hurt, exactly, but the sensation took adjusting to. He withdrew his thumb and caressed my ass again. Then he leaned down, put his tongue to the top of my cleft and licked me up my entire spine. Reaching the top, he clamped his hot mouth to the base of my neck. Electric sparks shot down my spinal cord and my toes curled.

"Wait," I rasped. I shimmied as close to the edge of the couch as I could get and reached down for my jeans.

"What is it you are looking for?"

"My phone is in my back pocket."

"You want that infernal thing *now?*"

"If I don't want my mother to freak out when she finds me missing tomorrow morning, then yes. Unless you're one of those guys who doesn't like actually sleeping with his conquests and you plan to kick me out when we're done."

He looked affronted. "I am *not* 'one of those guys.' And I most definitely will not be kicking you out." He bent down, rummaged in the pile of our discarded clothing, and found my phone. "Go ahead, reassure your *maman.*"

I would catch hell in the morning from Mom, but I no longer cared. I was a grown woman, not a recalcitrant teenager. I composed a text while Luc disposed of his used rubber. He reached into the little jar on the end table and pulled another one out. Having sent my message, I turned my head and watched him take his now flaccid cock in his hand, priming himself for whatever he had planned next.

Seeing me watching, he slowed his massaging, and his lips crooked upwards. "I like when you watch me."

I caught my breath at the hunger in his eyes. He closed his and arched his back slightly, his cock engorging itself beneath his strong, methodical fingers. Finally, he slipped on the condom.

He pivoted and crawled on top of me, his thighs to either side of mine, his not quite fully hardened shaft laid along the cleft of my ass and his sack tickling the base of my buttocks.

I tensed again, unsure of his intentions. "I've never—"

"Shhh, *mignonne*. That is not what I had in mind." He laid both hands on my lower back and started to massage me with deep strokes, working his way up the muscles of my back with rhythmic deliberation, using his weight to relax any kinks he found. His hips pushed in time with the pressure of his hands, rocking mine deep into the couch cushion. I closed my eyes as the tension of uncertainty drained from me, and a different kind of tension took its place.

His hands reached my shoulders and he draped the entire length of his body along my frame. "Tell me if I become too heavy." He let his full weight press down on me, and I sighed. He slid a hand beneath me and cupped my breast, the heat of his palm so welcome against my nipple. His laid his cheek next to mine and our breath mingled.

His hips still rocked me slowly back and forth. His cock grew larger and harder between my cheeks. I tilted my ass up a bit to meet him, wanting more. This time he obliged me without teasing, withdrawing his hand from beneath me in order to guide himself into me. I spread my legs for him and he found me still wet and ready from our previous bout as he slid into me, not quite as deep because of our prone position.

Just by my head, he pressed his palm against the back of my hand, twining his fingers with mine. He wedged his other hand beneath me again, this time cupping my pubis, his fingers just at the top of my crease.

Then he rocked, a small movement, his cock sliding back and forth just enough to create a pleasant friction. He added a slight circular motion to his undulation as he clasped my hand tightly and pressed my hips to his with his other hand.

We spent long minutes like this, and I grew almost hypnotized. I'd gotten my earlier wish, to be encased by him and to encase him, and it was wondrous. The rocking lulled me, our breathing synchronized, the heat of our connected bodies bathing me in luxurious intimacy. It was pure physical contentment, until it became more.

Our skin grew slippery with sweat. He nuzzled my cheek, then planted hot wet kisses below my ear and down my shoulder. I tilted my ass up more, resisting his weight, craving him deep inside me, deeper than the gentle rocking allowed. My cunt tensed, and he inhaled sharply. His hand down low slid between my thighs, and he plunged his fingers into my folds, still rocking his hips, a little faster now, never relenting.

His fingers slicked me, rubbing to either side of my clit. I moaned, unable to escape, not wanting to escape, but craving a release he was in no hurry to give me. His mouth found mine and I whimpered softly against his tongue, lapping mine against it. And still he rocked, his body hard and unyielding on top of mine, maintaining that implacable rhythm.

The pressure built within me, and my clit pulsed beneath his fingers, straining out of its hood. I moaned with each breath as his cock slid back and forth, trying to arch my back, tilting my pelvis against his weight, desperate now to engulf him deep within me.

Suddenly he let go of my hand, pushed himself up and grabbed my hip. Freed from the pressure of his body atop mine, I slid my ass back and up with him, crying out as he finally thrust fully inside me. I buried my face in the sofa. His fingers rubbed my engorged nub. I shuddered with pleasure. His shaft scraped against my inner walls and now his thrusts deepened, his sack slapping against me with each drive forward. The wet sucking sounds of his fingers working my cunt and his cock sliding in and out filled the spaces between my own moans.

"Nadia," he breathed. He circled his fingers around and across my clit, stretching the skin, setting all my nerve endings afire. "Come for me."

I rammed my ass against his hips, reached a hand between my legs. To his deep massage I added a fluttering index finger across the very tip of my nub. And then I screamed as fiery pleasure burst from my core and up the base of my spine.

Luc slammed into me, groaning as my orgasm ripped through me and my cunt clenched around his cock, bringing him to his own climax. He twitched inside me as the sublime sensation coursing through me dissipated. He slid out of me and trailed his hands along my heaving flanks, bent forward, and rubbed my shoulders. "And now, *chaton? Es-tu finalement rassasiée?"*

I twisted beneath him until I was lying on my back, reached up, and yanked him down to me, crushing his mouth with mine. "You magnificent man," I murmured against his cheek when I broke off.

"I will take that as a yes." He kissed me back, his tongue lingering inside my mouth. We both smiled contented smiles against each other's lips. He dropped down beside me and pulled a throw from the back of the sofa, draping it over the two of us, and collecting me inside his snug embrace. My breathing slowed, his breath warm against my cheek, and I let myself drift off into dreams of tangled limbs and crooked grins.

CHAPTER ELEVEN

I woke to the rich aroma of espresso and hot croissants. Outside the window, a car honked. Luc was no longer spooning against me, but had thoughtfully left a robe draped over the couch. I shrugged it on and padded towards the tempting smells emanating from the kitchen.

I found Luc seated in a sunny breakfast nook, studying his laptop and sipping coffee. I made a beeline for the coffee machine. Luc pushed back his chair, stood, and came up behind me, wrapping me in a hug and nuzzling my hair. "You slept well?"

"I did." I leaned back into him, enjoying the feel of his arms around me. My body had taken no time learning how to miss him. I studied the knobs and switches on the espresso maker, trying to figure out which configuration would get me liquid energy fastest. Luc let me stew for thirty seconds then took pity on me. He disengaged from me, then released the coffee basket, dumped out the old grounds, tamped in some new ones, and fired up the pump. Within ninety seconds I was gratefully sipping from my own cup.

Some of my torpor from last night still lingered, but just the sight of Luc this morning had set my spine tingling and a warmth brewing in my loins. I admired his ass—trim but well-defined—as he bent down to retrieve a croissant for me from his oven. "They are fresh from the *boulangerie* at the corner. I was keeping them warm for you." He handed me a plate and we both sat in the nook, not saying much as I tore into the flakey, buttery pastry.

I wasn't sure what to say, where we went from here, what his expectations might be. He'd rescued me from my own lie, creating something true from falsehood. And then given me better sex than I'd had in I didn't know how long. Was this the start of something special or would it be over as soon as Mom left?

Luc broke the silence first, taking the tack I least expected. "Does she always speak to you that way?"

"Who, my mother?"

Luc nodded.

"You mean, like an incompetent child?"

"I would not have put it quite that way, but yes."

I sighed. "I grew up in a very conservative household. Then became an art major. And an atheist." There's nothing like the arts community to deprogram you from religious fundamentalism. "My mother is an expert at finding unique ways to voice her passive-aggressive disapproval of all my lifestyle choices." I had a great education, a good job history —if not a great income history—but I hadn't settled down and popped out kids like a good little minister's daughter, much to Mom's consternation and perpetual disappointment. "I cope with it mostly via avoidance."

"I see."

"I mean, don't get me wrong. I love my mother. I just don't like her very much." I'd kind of thrown in the towel on ever changing her attitude. Dad was no help, always distant, preferring to avoid conflict rather than air out our family issues. Which was incredibly frustrating given his ministry and supposed position as the parish's conscience and moral center. How many families had he advised while ours soldiered on amid simmering grievances? "I should warn you, dysfunction is my family's middle name. If you want to call last night a fun little lark and move on, I won't think any less of you. Mom doesn't expect any of my relationships to last, so your sudden departure will be easy to explain."

I realized how pathetically awful that sounded as soon as I said it.

Luc reached out for my hand, his thumb stroking my knuckles, his eyes serious for once. "Why not take things as they come, for now? After all, I am the one who imposed myself on you."

"Luc—" My voice caught at the back of my throat, but I had to get the next words out. "At first I took this for a slightly annoying prank. But don't ever think that you've been any kind of imposition to me. Last night …" I blinked away the moisture that suddenly threatened to spill from the corner of my eyes. "Last night is something I'll never forget, no matter what happens, and I need you to know how grateful I am."

Because it hadn't been just great sex. It had been intimacy, a kind of connection I hadn't known I was missing. And even if Luc disappeared from my life tomorrow, I now understood how much I'd cut myself off from my own life, and letting others into it. I'd *enjoyed* Luc. And he had enjoyed me. It was no more complicated than that, and that was a revelation. I didn't intend to become the Queen of One-Night Stands, but there was a balance between that and walling myself off like I'd done since I broke up with Ben.

Luc reached across the table, scrubbing his fingers through my tangled hair. He pulled me gently toward him, and kissed my forehead. "I am glad, *chaton*. Life is too short for regrets."

He opened a small box on the table and plucked out a chocolate truffle powdered in cocoa. "And life is too short to start the day without *chocolat*. Come and get your treat." He placed the chocolate between his lips and crooked his finger. I leaned into him, bit the little round ball in half, letting the rich ganache melt, swirling it off his tongue, trying to get more than my fair share. He licked the cocoa from my lips.

"Now that's a morning tradition I can get behind."

Luc stood and put his coffee cup in the sink. "*Écoute*, I must leave you. I have an early meeting. I left you towels for the shower. Stay as long as you like, the door locks automatically."

I glanced at the time, stood as well. "I have to get to work too. And let Mom know I'm alive."

Luc grinned. "She will think I ravished you."

I sidled up to him and put my arms around his waist. "You can ravish me any time."

He took my face between his palms and kissed me. I opened my mouth to his and drew his tongue in, trying to memorize the taste of him, all chocolate and coffee. He pressed against me and his hard bulge warmed the silk of the robe against my belly. He withdrew from my mouth, his lips playing lightly with mine before he released me. "I will be happy to oblige. But sadly, duty calls."

I stepped back, my hands trailing along his hips, my fingers giving that bulge a mischievous caress. "Have a lovely day. Think naughty thoughts of me."

Desire flashed in the green depths of Luc's eyes and his lips crooked. "I have created a little monster, it seems."

"No regrets, though."

"*Jamais.*" And with a wry smile he turned and left me in an apartment that suddenly felt too big without him.

I wandered off in search of that shower. Made sure it erred towards the cold side.

CHAPTER TWELVE

I made it in to work only a few minutes late—not that the boss was a stickler for punctuality—after showering and locating some mouthwash in Luc's medicine cabinet. My clothing was in acceptable shape because I'd changed after work last night before dinner.

Amélie was waiting for me at my desk with a café au lait, her first day back from the Louvre. "So? How was your dinner?"

"Dinners, actually."

"*Oh la la, c'est sérieux.*"

"Mom was sufficiently bamboozled."

"Bamboozled?"

"She bought the ruse."

"I see. And you? I should have warned you. Luc used to be a *grand séducteur.*"

A hot flush spread across my cheeks and down my chest. "*Used* to be?"

Amélie clapped a hand to her mouth. "*Non.*" She stared

at me. Squealed. "*Oui!* But with your mother there?"

"I … succumbed to his charms, yes. But not at my place."

"He can be *très charmant.*" What an understatement. Amélie shimmied excitedly. "But this is *fantastique!* Luc is a really nice guy. How do you say? A big softie. Did you know he introduced me to Chloë?"

I shook my head. "For a guy whose master seducer days are supposedly behind him, he moves pretty fast."

"When we were in school, he was always with someone different. But lately, he's slowed down. His past few relationships were pretty serious. But the last one ended badly. He has not spoken of anyone new since." She bounced up and down a little. "Oh, I am so happy for you both."

"It's a little early to read too much into this."

"It does not matter. It's still so much fun. Chloë will be *mort de rire.*"

I took a sip of my cooling coffee. I suppose the whole thing *was* pretty funny when viewed from a certain angle.

CHAPTER THIRTEEN

AFTER work I took Mom out for dinner at a bistro around the corner from my place. One cooking misadventure was quite enough for me, thank you. And without Luc to backstop me, I didn't feel like risking my newly found equanimity on squabbles I could avoid.

I'd spent the day shaking myself out of daydreams of him. I had work to do, but memories of the previous evening kept intruding at inopportune times. I'd completely missed a question posed to me by my boss in our afternoon status meeting because my brain put on loop the feel of Luc's lips on my breasts. Amélie had had to kick my ankle to snap me back to attention.

"Did you have a good time today?" I speared a scallop from the shell plate of my coquille St-Jacques, reminding myself of my daughterly duty.

"Yes. I strolled along the banks of the Seine, took that boat tour I was thinking about, and went up the Eiffel Tower."

"You didn't go to the Moulin Rouge?" I teased.

"You know I'm not one for bawdy houses, Nadia."

"It hasn't been infamous for that type of thing in decades, Mom."

"Still. Morals must be upheld. Speaking of which …"

Oh, here we go.

"I presume you stayed at Luc's last night."

"Mom, I'm a grown woman. Who no longer subscribes to outdated, puritanical notions of what's proper between two people in a relationship."

"But I believe differently, and I would have thought that while I was here you'd at least respect that."

In other words, *what I don't see doesn't hurt me.* "Mom. I don't have that much time left in Paris—"

"And you haven't been here that long either. Aren't you two moving a little quickly?"

If she only knew just how quickly we'd moved. Her words reminded me that I *was* lying to her, after all—never a good look on a daughter. I took a sip of wine, not sure how to reply.

"Do you love him, at least?"

"It's too early to say that."

"Oh, Nadia. Sex without love is just …"

"… really good sex, Mom." I bit back a jab about love without sex, because that would have been hitting below the belt. Mom and Dad had maintained separate rooms for years.

She pursed her lips and stabbed a piece of steak. "You loved Ben. I don't understand why you two couldn't make things work."

I let my fork fall to the table with a clatter. "Don't you dare. Don't you dare throw Ben in my face. You of all people."

Mom wouldn't meet my eyes. "You were such a good match."

"Mom—"

"He was good for you, admit it."

"He *lied* to me."

"But it was a lie in service of a greater good."

"A lie *you* concocted!"

"We just had your best interests at heart."

"Our whole relationship was based on a … a setup. A false premise."

My nostrils still flared at the memory.

"You're going to hold that over me forever, aren't you?" Mom asked.

So much for avoidance. Fine. It was time we fully had this one out. "And why wouldn't I, Mom? Why do you think I haven't dated anyone since? It couldn't possibly be because I have trouble trusting men now, could it?" I took a big gulp of my wine. "You and Dad *still* haven't apologized."

"Because there's nothing to apologize for. We were trying to do right by you."

"I'm not chattel, Mom. If you can't see how basing a relationship on openness and trust might be important, then I can't help you." The fight went out of me as quickly as it had flared. It was no use arguing. I would never get a concession from her. Just more guilt. I signaled the waiter for *l'addition*.

"But I haven't finished my steak."

"Take your time. I'm afraid I've lost my appetite. Have you got my spare key with you?"

"Yes."

"Great." I paid the bill then shouldered on my jacket. "Don't forget tomorrow's the day I'm showing you around." Because *that* was going to be a barrel of laughs. "I'll see you in the morning."

I was tired of always being in the wrong in her eyes. Of being made to feel that toeing the family line was more important than my own needs. If she'd even remotely acknowledged how her actions had hurt me, I might have softened. But apparently a lifetime of preaching had left her with an inability to listen.

The irony that my current relationship was also based on a false premise wasn't lost on me. The difference was I'd known about this one from the start.

CHAPTER FOURTEEN

BREAKFAST the next morning was a tense, quiet affair, Mom steering clear of any whiff of talk about relationships. Thankfully, Luc had texted me last night and offered to tour us through one of his former projects, a refurbished mansion that had been converted into a museum of couture throughout the ages. With the help of his buffering presence, I might just be able to make it through the day without blowing up at Mom again.

We met him by the ticketing counter, and we did the French double cheek-buss in greeting. I rented Mom the headphones for the self-guided tour. I preferred to keep my ears free for conversation with Luc.

The museum was cleverly laid out, with each room decorated in the style of its era, from the early Middle Ages through the Renaissance, latter centuries of the last millennium, and on through the decades of the twentieth and twenty-first centuries. Mannequins sat or stood posed in scenes of daily life, wearing the clothing of their day. Vibrant silks and taffetas contrasted with linens and sturdier work cloth, a range of textiles, embroidery patterns, and lace on display. Mom gravitated towards the fanciest traditional gowns.

"If we get separated, we'll meet by the gift shop, OK?"

Mom nodded, waved, and wandered off towards the Chanel room, engrossed in her audio. Luc and I followed a few paces behind. We passed a doorway and Luc tugged me inside. I found myself surrounded by corsets, bustles, petticoats, and other undergarments. Luc pulled me deeper into rooms that displayed the history of lingerie, from the first closed-crotch underwear—which apparently wasn't *de rigueur* for women before the late nineteenth century—to slips, bras, and teddies.

He paused by a paneled wall, watching the only other couple in the room until they moved out of view. Then he pressed his fingers against a square of wood, which popped into the wall. He slid it aside, quickly operated some sort of latch within, and the entire wall panel hinged inward.

"*Vite.*" He shepherded me inside and closed the door behind him. "They had us build a secret room. It's only for special tours. Contributes to the mystique."

We were in what I could only characterize as a boudoir, with crimson wallpaper and dark wood paneling. Latex catsuits and leather fetish gear adorned the mannequins, with a female form dressed in strips of rubber posed on the bed. "Should we be in here?"

"Probably not. But that is half the fun." He pushed me

up against a heavy oak sideboard displaying crops and cuffs, and slid his hand along the side of my neck, ran his nose along my cheek. "You would look so sexy in some of these items, *chaton*. Last night, I let my imagination go wild." He pressed his crotch against mine. "You see? It makes me hard just to think of it."

My breath came faster. "Aren't there security cameras in here?"

He glanced up towards the far corner. "Being the designer has some privileges. I have friends in high places. As long as we do not disturb the displays, no one need ever know." I followed his gaze. A black cloth hung from a squarish shape—presumably the camera—near the ceiling moldings. He'd planned ahead.

I turned my face back to him, brushed my lips against his, intrigued but tentative. I'd never contemplated anything this wanton before. I could just hear what my mother would say if she found out. Decidedly unsexy, that voice in my head. "What if someone comes in?"

"There is no reward without risk, *chérie*. Indulge my little carnal *fantaisie*. Must I beg?" He traced a finger down my throat, along the V of my blouse, sneaking it beneath the cup of my bra to lightly tease my nipple. My peak tightened instantly.

All thought of propriety fled. "Fuck I want you." I mashed my mouth against his. My tongue sought his out, hot, greedy, and ravenous. I needed him right fucking now, my ferocious desire overwhelming all common sense. He clutched my ass and lifted me onto the sideboard, his tongue jousting with mine.

Furious, impatient lust displaced the other evening's languid foreplay. He ruched up my skirt while I tore at the button of his pants. He stripped me of my panties, ran covetous fingers through my slit, groaning when he found me wet and straining against his palm. I freed his cock from his briefs. He reached into his breast pocket, whipped out a condom wrapper, and tore it open. I snatched it from him, hastily sheathed him, and guided him between my legs.

He took me in one quick thrust, and I arched, wrapping my thighs around his waist. Clasping his back, I pressed my face to his shoulder. My teeth dug into his shirt to stifle my moans as he speared me. We rutted—that was the only word for it—fast and hard and feral.

The threat of discovery heightened all my senses as I rode him like the thoroughbred lover he was. His cock pounded my clit, the only sound our ragged panting and wet noises from our joined loins.

Were those footsteps in the room on the other side of the wall? I tensed.

Luc took my face in his hands, his eyes boring into mine. "There is only us. Only this now."

He impaled me—skewered and gored me with his look and his cock, and I came in a great wracking torrent. I threw my head back and opened my mouth in a long, hoarse gasp. Luc pressed his mouth to the crook of my neck, his searing tongue at my jugular. His hips jerked in answer and he brought himself off some seconds later as I shuddered and clenched around him and panted against his chest, gripping his shirt to keep from flopping against the wall.

When we could both breathe again, he lifted my chin until I was looking at him, and caressed my cheek. "Ah, *ma petite rareté*. What a wonder you are." He kissed the bridge of my nose, then sighed. "But we have probably been gone long enough for your *maman* to notice."

He slid out of me while I slipped off the sideboard, reaching for my shoulder bag, which had fallen to the floor. I found some tissue inside, offered him a few sheets, then cleaned myself off and shimmied back into my underwear while he dealt with tidying himself up, the mannequin on the bed our only witness.

Seeing I was ready, Luc cracked open the hidden door. He motioned me through when the coast was clear, and we strode back out from the more staid lingerie exhibits into the main corridor. Luc discreetly tossed the tissue-wrapped condom into a convenient bin just as we reached the gift shop. I browsed the shelves, not really seeing the knickknacks for sale, as I waited for Mom to find us.

I felt lascivious and strange, voluptuous and lewd, like I'd just transgressed against the final constraints of my upbringing.

I didn't regret a second of it.

CHAPTER FIFTEEN

"WHY don't we lunch at a little café I know near here?" Luc squeezed my hand.

"That sounds lovely." Mom stashed the printed scarf she'd purchased at the gift shop in her purse. "I'm famished."

"They have croque-monsieurs and great charcuterie plates. And good beer. Come." He wrapped his arm around my waist as we headed off down the street, and I smiled a secret smile. He was everything Ben was not, the opposite of what Ben represented in my head—a man who wanted me for me, not because I got him something else. A man willing to give all of himself with abandon, with no expectations in return. I finally felt free of that horrible baggage, like I was a thousand pounds lighter. I hadn't even realized how much it had weighed me down.

The art deco café was bustling with the lunch crowd, but we snagged a table as another group of diners left.

"So you designed that place?" Mom sipped her pilsner.

"Not the exhibits. But the building itself was almost

falling down—they very nearly demolished it—and the museum hired my firm to rescue it."

"Neat."

He was good with Mom, keeping the conversation away from me and on safe topics like her sightseeing. It was too bad he was busy this afternoon, because after lunch, I'd have to entertain her myself. I gathered my new, carefree mood around me like a suit of armor, determined to keep the last part of her stay here harmonious.

I dug into my crêpe florentine, our little escapade at the museum having stimulated my appetite in addition to my libido. Luc made small talk with Mom as I ate and listened and interjected every now and then. He shot sly glances my way, reminders of our illicit little tryst, and I struggled not to fan myself. He laid a hand on the table next to mine, brushed my pinky with his, and quirked his lips in amusement.

A shadow loomed over our table and I looked up, expecting the waiter. A tall, buff man with blond hair and a hard, chiseled face stood between Luc's and my chairs, staring down at our touching hands.

"*Luc? C'est qui ces gens là?*"

Luc paled, stood up. "*Mathieu. C'est une amie et sa mère.*" His tone was flat, dismissive.

"*Je croyais que tu étais fini avec les femmes.*" Oh dear. This must be Luc's ex. The one Amélie said hadn't ended well.

Luc rolled his eyes. "*Tu te flattes.*"

Mom leaned towards me. "Who is that?"

I couldn't look away from Luc and Mathieu. "I think it's

an old friend of Luc's."

"He doesn't sound very friendly."

Mathieu's tone was low and dangerous. "*Tu me manques.*"

"*Pas içi.*" Luc hissed.

"*Où, d'abord? Tu ne retourne pas mes appels.*"

"*Je t'ai dit que c'était fini entre nous.*"

"*C'est* moi *qui décidera lorsque c'est fini.*" Mathieu grabbed Luc by the jaw and smashed his mouth against Luc's. He forced Luc's jaw open, rough and possessive, tongued him messily. A pall of silence fell over the tables around us.

Luc pushed Mathieu away. "*Es-tu malade?*"

Without thinking, I stepped between the two men.

Mathieu sneered at me, then laughed in Luc's face. "*Tu laisses ta putaine te défendre?* Tell your American whore to go home."

"I'm not American, asshole." I quivered with indignation and false bravado.

"No matter. You should leave before you get hurt. *Pute.*" Mathieu whipped around and stalked out of the café.

The conversations around us resumed, slightly hushed now, with our neighbors casting covert glances at our little dramatic tableau. Luc's hands gripped the back of his chair, his knuckles white. I reached out to touch his elbow, and he snapped his gaze back to me from his fixation on the door.

"Who was that?" Mom's voice quavered.

"I'm sorry." Luc scrubbed his face with his palm. "That was my ex." He took my hand, rubbed his other one along my upper arm. "Are you all right?"

"DON'T YOU TOUCH HER."

I stared at Mom, shocked. Luc froze.

"Get your filthy hands off my daughter, you pervert!"

Someone gasped. You could hear a pin drop in the restaurant.

"Mother!"

"Get away from him, Nadia."

"I most certainly will not. Apologize to Luc, Mom. *Now.*" The anger I'd felt for Mathieu paled in comparison to the outrage coursing through me now.

"I will do no such thing. He's an abomination. Sullied in the eyes of God."

Luc let go of my hand. "Nadia," he said softly. "Please." Stricken wasn't an expression that belonged on Luc's face.

"No, Luc. This is wrong. I won't let her treat you this way."

He gathered up his jacket, shrugged it on. "You cannot help that your mother is a bigot. I'm sorry. I must leave." He pulled some Euro notes from his wallet and tossed them on the table. "I would like to say it was a pleasure meeting you, Madame Fisker, but I would be lying. Goodbye, Nadia." And with that, he was just gone.

I couldn't even look at my mother. I stormed over to the cash. "*L'addition, s'il vous plait.*" I took out my credit card with trembling fingers, paid the whole bill, leaving Luc's cash on the table as an extra-large tip to try to make up for the scene we'd caused. Then I marched out of the restaurant, leaving my mother to deal with the stares of the other customers however she saw fit.

Hot tears burned my eyes, tears of rage and sorrow both, and I didn't know for whom I felt worse, me or Luc. There was no way to ever apologize for what my mother had just said. Shame slithered through me. And to think once I might have felt more ashamed about what I'd done with Luc at the museum earlier.

That was nothing compared to this.

CHAPTER SIXTEEN

By the time Mom's key rattled in the lock, I'd moved her suitcase from the bedroom to the couch, and swept the bathroom for her toiletries and dumped them on the coffee table.

White-hot anger still churned through me, but I was prepared to try to talk to her if she showed even the slightest bit of contrition.

But she thrust her chin out, looking more self-righteous than ever. "You're relegating me to the couch?"

Not even a hint of an apology. That settled that. "No, Mom." I tossed a scrap of paper onto her suitcase. "I've booked you a hotel room for the rest of your stay. There's the address and booking confirmation."

"You'd kick out your own mother?"

"You invaded my home without warning or invitation, and then you insulted—no, *degraded* my friend in public, when he's shown you nothing but kindness and courtesy. It's beyond the fucking pale, Mom."

"Don't use that language with me."

"Then maybe you shouldn't have used such vile language with Luc."

"I was protecting you!"

"From *what?* He's been nothing but wonderful to me. Despite the fact that he's not even really my boyfriend."

"What?"

"We made it all up. Because he didn't want me to get caught in a lie."

"Why would you lie about that?"

"So you'd leave me alone, Mom. So you wouldn't try to set me up with another Ben. God, this is so messed up."

"But you spent the night with him! And after knowing him"—I could see her reviewing the week in her head—"for only two days! It's—"

"What, Mom? A sin? A black mark on my immortal soul? I don't care. Luc's amazing."

She scoffed. "You can't change him you know. That kind never changes."

I threw up my hands in exasperation. "That '*kind?*' I don't *want* to change him. He's perfectly fine the way he is."

"If this was all just an act, then you can't even say 'what way' he is. You can't be sure of anything about him. Did you even know about that man who—who *kissed* him?" Mom's lip curled. "It's a good thing I intervened before things got too far. It's all worked out for the best."

"What makes you think it's over?" She was probably right, but I refused to admit it.

"Really Nadia, you can't seriously want to pursue a relationship with this—this person." She said "person" like she'd smelled a rotting carcass.

"I don't think I've ever wanted anything more."

"Don't you see? I don't want you to get hurt. I don't want this for you."

"What about what *I* want? Why can't you just let me live my own life?"

Her face crumpled. "Because the way you're going, you'll wind up just like *me!*" She sagged onto the arm of the couch, buried her head in her hands.

I went still. Remembered the unusual drinking when she'd arrived. The heightened brittleness. "Why are you really here, Mom?"

She dashed brusquely at her eyes. "Your father's not at the convocation of ministers. He left me." She spat out her next words. "For a man."

A whole lot of weirdness about my parents' marriage snapped into crisp focus. The separate bedrooms. The avoidance of intimacy. The evangelical hysteria about queerness.

"He's renounced the faith. Abdicated his ministry. He's turned us into pariahs in the church."

"How long have you suspected he was gay?" Because she couldn't have lived with him for over thirty years and been that blind, could she?

"I—from the beginning."

"And you married him anyway?"

"My father … had been grooming David to take over the ministry. When David expressed his doubts to him, confessed his sinful thoughts, your grandfather assured him he could cure him, save his soul from the devil."

Nausea roiled my stomach.

Mom continued. "We'd already been seeing each other. My father said it was my duty as a Christian to help David on his road to recovery. That if he was in a good marriage, with a good Christian woman, he wouldn't be tempted to backslide." She shrugged. "You know the rest."

I'd never heard anything more appalling in my life. I mean, I'd heard of conversion therapy, grown up steeped in the fundie propaganda of my family's evangelical sect, but never in a million years had I suspected that they'd inflicted such garbage on each other. I'd thought they were mostly full of self-righteous talk. But now I knew better—that talk and words led to actual harm.

I closed my eyes and took some deep, calming breaths. Part of me ached for Mom and Dad and the pain they'd caused each other. Another part of me raged at the deep injustice my family's misguided moralizing had inflicted in ever-widening ripples around them.

I tried to keep my voice level. I could use my own words to try to make Mom see, but she hadn't shown herself to be in any frame of mind to listen. I still wasn't going to abdicate my responsibility here. I had to believe words mattered. That truth mattered.

"Mom. Luc's not Dad. And I'm not you. I'm sorry for

what you and Dad have been through, and I'm sorry your marriage is over. I think you need—you both need—to talk to a good therapist. And not someone in the church. That shit's messed up." I scrubbed my palm through my hair. "It's so messed up that it's left you with a twisted idea of what love should be. I don't believe the things you believe. And if your vision of love entails forcing someone to deny who they are, and you can't see how wrong that is, then I need you to leave. Leave my home. And maybe—for now—leave my life."

"Nadia … you can't mean that."

"I can. And I do."

"You've known him for less than a week! You'd choose him over me? I'm your *mother!*"

"You may have birthed me, but right now, you're no mother to me. Just go. Write to me when you're ready to apologize." I turned my back on her and locked myself in the bedroom.

"Nadia!" She pounded on the door for a few minutes, pleading with me to reconsider, but I ignored her. After a while, I heard her moving around the living room, gathering her things. When the front door clicked shut behind her, I opened the bedroom door cautiously to make sure she was gone.

Then I went to the bathroom and threw up.

CHAPTER SEVENTEEN

BY Monday, I hadn't heard back from Luc, despite sending him several texts and leaving him a voicemail apology. Over our mid-morning coffee break, I told Amélie what had happened.

"Wow. That's *complètement fucké.*"

I laughed without mirth. "I don't even know if I did the right thing, shutting her out like that." My stomach was still doing flip-flops.

"It sounds to me like nothing less would get through to her." I'd told Amélie about Ben as well.

"But isn't dialogue better?"

"You told her what you needed to start a dialogue. Now the *ballon* is in her court. What about your father?"

Yeah, good old Dad. Who hadn't even bothered to call to let me know he'd abandoned Mom. "I don't know. I guess I'll talk to him at some point." I didn't know how to untangle the mess of emotions that jangled through me at the thought. "Could I ask you for a favor?"

"Anything."

"I haven't been able to reach Luc, and I … don't want to presume to understand what he's going through, or … intrude on that any more than I have with the messages I've left him. What Mom said to him was … shit … I don't want to leave things with him on such a fucked up note." I toyed with the handle of my coffee mug. "Would you just let him know that if he can stand the sight of me, I'll be in the *Nymphéas* exhibit at the Musée de l'Orangerie after work on Friday?" Maybe with almost a week of distance from this weekend's events, some of the bad taste might have faded away.

"I will try."

"Great."

Amélie stood up. "By the way, Madame Chastain asked to see you this afternoon."

The head of the AAS. Maybe she wanted to go over my interim internship evaluation. "OK. Tell her I'll pop in."

I could use a distraction from my churning postconflict feelings.

CHAPTER EIGHTEEN

THE clock ticked inexorably towards closing time, and still no Luc. I sat on a bench, staring at the immense mural in front of me, letting my eyes defocus a little until the blues and greens and pinks and lavenders blurred even further than Monet's impressionistic brush strokes intended. I could almost hear a fish splash and a frog croak, the buzzing of dragonflies on a warm summer day.

Someone sat down on the bench beside me without saying a word. I snuck a glance to my right.

The silence stretched to sixty seconds. Ninety.

"I usually feel so serene in this room," I said.

"But not today," Luc replied.

"No. Not today."

Still he just sat there.

"You know how you're not the kind of guy who kicks a girl out after a night of great sex?"

Luc snorted.

"Well, apparently I'm the kind of girl who kicks her

mother out after an afternoon of awful words."

"They were pretty vile, yes."

"They were unforgivable."

Luc twisted to face me. "I do understand that you are not your mother, you know. I just wish, when you'd told me your parents were conservative, you'd explained just *how* conservative. Canada is supposed to be so liberal."

Especially the West Coast, where I grew up. But just outside anything-goes Vancouver, pockets of evangelical Christianity and streaks of ultra-conservatism lurked in places like the bedroom community where I'd been raised. "I'm sorry. For everything. You'd suggested taking things as they came, she was only staying for a few days, and I figured it was unlikely to matter. If you and I wound up getting closer, I would have told you. And I would have found a way of broaching the topic with Mom in a less … dramatic context. Which isn't to say she would have reacted any better, but at least she wouldn't have done it in front of fifty other people."

Luc glanced at his watch. "The museum is closing. Walk with me?"

We stood and exited the building, then strolled through the Jardins des Tuileries.

"Is she gone, then?"

I shrugged. "I don't know. Her original flight was supposed to leave on Wednesday. But I haven't spoken to her since Saturday. I told her I wouldn't until she apologized."

We found the treed promenade along the banks of the Seine. Luc leaned his elbows on the stone parapet and stared down at the green water flowing past. "This thing with your mother. It is bad. I am unfortunately accustomed to dealing with people such as her. But it is not why I did not call you."

"I don't understand."

"I do not hold you responsible for your mother's words. But Mathieu …" Luc looked up at the sky, then back down to me. "Mathieu worried me."

Ah. "Amélie told me it was a difficult parting."

"I ended it two months ago and had not spoken to him since. And yet he still—" Luc shook his head. "Well, you saw. He is incredibly possessive. Which is why I stopped seeing him. His *jalousie* … he would sulk and not speak to me for days if I so much as looked at someone else. I refused to live that way."

I wanted to reach out and put a comforting hand on his arm, but wasn't sure of my welcome.

"Had I known he had still not moved on I would have … I don't know, but I should have warned you. What he did in the restaurant—it was ugly, and not fair to you."

"Luc …" This time I did reach out, squeezed his hand. "You couldn't have known we'd run into him."

"No. But I needed to speak to him. To disabuse him of this notion that things were not finished between us."

"And did you?"

Luc nodded. "I was firm, and I think he understood. But I cannot be sure he does not still cling to the hope I will come back to him. I just … do not want him to take his frustrations out on you. He can be … persistent. Perhaps it would be best if you stayed away from me until I resolve this."

"Is Mathieu dangerous?"

"*Non, non.* He was never physically violent. That does not mean he is incapable of hurtful words or creating another scene. It is probably *un drame* you do not need right now."

I gazed down at my hand on his, marshaling my thoughts, picking up the shattered pieces of last week's newfound lightness of spirit and experimentally gluing a few of them back together in my head. Luc didn't hate me. He was worried for me. I tilted my head up to meet his eyes. "You said you refused to live like that. But if you push me away aren't you giving Mathieu exactly what he wants?"

"*Ah, chaton …*" He looked away. "Are you not leaving in a few weeks anyway?"

How many echoes of other lovers' questions—their hopes and fears—had the waters of this river carried away across the years? My own hopes lifted at Luc's wistful tone. I shoved my fears into the past where they belonged.

I fidgeted, still a little uncertain of my footing. "We-ell … about that … My boss just offered me a permanent position. I'd need to see if my faculty adviser will let me work on my thesis remotely but … I was thinking of staying on." I wasn't particularly tempted to return to British Columbia and the ruins of my family life.

Luc met my gaze again, green eyes as limpid as a forest stream.

"I … like it here. I like the job, and jobs for art history

majors are few and far between, believe me. I love the food. And the wine. The cigarette smoke not so much. But the people make up for that." I rubbed his hand, stroked the ridges of his tendons. "Maybe … certain people more than others."

"Even people with troublesome exes?" He turned his hand over to clasp my fingers. "What of your family?"

"I have a cousin I think you'd really like."

"I am serious. You would risk your entire relationship with your parents over me?"

"That relationship was already broken, this just helped me admit that it's not mine to fix. I spent the better part of a year walling myself off from other relationships to minimize my risk of getting hurt again." I squeezed Luc's fingers. "A certain someone recently convinced me there's a better way. You're the first person in a very long time …" My voice cracked a little. "… who seems to care just as much about my happiness as their own. If that's not worth some risk, I don't know what is. To hell with safe."

And there it was, just a twitch, a hint of an upward tilt at the corner of his mouth. "What are you saying, *chaton*?"

"I think I'm saying I'd like you to kiss me now."

"*Ça me fera infiniment plaisir, mon amour.*"

Then he gathered me in his arms, and I forgot about Mom, forgot about Mathieu, forgot about everything but the soft welcome of his lips and tongue as he kissed me until I almost forgot my own name.

A TASTE of Temptation

CHAPTER ONE

"YOU useless piece of—"

I kicked gravel at my bike's tire and whacked the side of the tank.

That would teach me to take the tiniest of tiny back roads. Diva, my aptly named motorcycle, squatted obliviously on the road and refused to start. I had plenty of fuel. There was no reason for her tantrum.

Of course, she'd picked the worst possible time. I'd been dawdling, having enjoyed a fantastic late-afternoon snack at a local monastery cum winery. *Be honest, El. You were procrastinating because you're not sure of your welcome.* I'd planned to arrive at Aunt Fran's some time around sunset. Given how late the Italians ate dinner, it shouldn't have been a problem.

But now the sun was dipping low, and I was in the middle of nowhere on the road less traveled, which meant walking to the nearest farmhouse in my gear to see if I could bum a jumpstart or a ride from some helpful soul.

I peeled off my riding gloves and pried my helmet off my

head, hooking it over one of the mirrors. Then I pushed the bike further to the side of the road. I dug out my cell phone, but coverage was nil, confirming my walk.

The summer heat started to get to me so I shrugged off my mesh jacket as well. It wouldn't fit in my crammed saddle bags, so I could either drape it over the seat and hope it didn't go AWOL while I hunted up help, or carry it with me. The road curved and dipped along the rolling Tuscan hills, and from here I couldn't tell how far I might have to trudge. I tied the jacket around my waist. That thing cost too much to just leave out for scavengers. I attached my helmet to the helmet lock for good measure.

"Time to start walking, El."

I grabbed the tank bag and took my own advice, slogging off in the direction I'd been originally going. I hadn't passed a building in over twenty minutes of riding, so figured I'd take my chances heading into the unknown. The GPS had claimed I was fairly close to my destination, but seven kilometers on foot would go far more slowly than I liked.

I'd been walking for twenty minutes without seeing any likely places to call at, building up a good sweat and a couple of blisters, when tires crunched on the road behind me. A small pickup truck pulled up beside me.

'È che la tua moto laggiù?'' A truly handsome man peered out the driver's side window. Dark hair—long on top and tousled by the wind, cut just to the ears—with sideburns and a heavy stubble framed high cheekbones and a square jaw with just the hint of a cleft. And those lips … Michelango

would have killed to sculpt those lips.

I remembered I'd been asked a question. "I'm sorry. I don't speak much Italian."

"Back there. It is your bike?"

"*Sì.*"

"You want me to take a look?"

"Do you know much about bikes?"

He shrugged. *"Un pochino."* He jerked his head at the passenger seat. "Get in."

I hesitated. A single woman, in a foreign country, getting into a car with a strange man. But my boots were definitely not made for walking, and he wasn't giving me any odd vibes. I might be too trusting but my instincts usually didn't steer me wrong.

"I don't bite, *straniera.*"

I trudged over to the passenger side. Trust him or walk for another hour—my feet chose for me.

I clambered up into the seat, and he held out his hand. "Vico."

"Pleased to meet you, Vico. I'm El."

"Ella?"

"No, El. Short for Élodie. Everybody just calls me El." Some people found it a bit of a mouthful, or misremembered it as Melody.

"I am not everyone, Elodia."

Well OK then. "Still. El is fine." Although Elodia had a lovely ring to it when he rolled it off his tongue like that.

Vico shrugged again, spun the wheel, and did a five-point

U-turn. He was wearing jeans and a dusty faded T-shirt that looked like it had spent the better part of its life outdoors. He had the well-muscled arms of a farmhand, a guess reinforced by the implements jangling around in the bed of the truck.

We reached the Diva in far less time than it had taken me to walk. Vico didn't say much during the drive, unusual in my limited experience with Italian men. He parked the truck in front of the bike and we both got out.

"I think it's bad fuel." That was my best guess. "I don't have a replacement filter with me, or the tools to get at the old one."

"It could be a loose ground. Try to start it?"

The engine didn't even cough when I pressed the ignition.

Vico rubbed his chin. "The battery is beneath the seat, *sì?*"

I nodded. It was worth a check. I lifted the seat and Vico examined the connections, but we got no joy when I tried starting the bike again.

Vico went to the bed of the truck and slid two aluminium struts down to make a ramp.

"You just carry a ramp around with you?"

"It is for deliveries."

I guess it was my lucky day.

We chivvied the Diva up into the bed of the truck—not an easy endeavor even with two people and the ramp—and Vico strapped it down. "Where are you going?"

"Near San Donato in Poggio."

Vico tilted his head. "It is where I live. You are hungry?

My nonna is making dinner. Better than hotel food."

"I wouldn't want to impose." They weren't expecting me at Fran's until tomorrow but I didn't think arriving early would cause any logistical issues. If Vico dropped me and the bike there, that would eliminate a lot of hassle for me. "I'm not at a hotel anyway."

"Still. Nonna's ragu is the best. You will eat, then I will take you where you need to go."

"I—"

"It is really not a problem. *Pero*, I need to eat before I move that bike again. It is *molto* heavy."

If it wasn't for the grandmother, I might think he was propositioning me. Not that I'd mind. He was decidedly easy to look at, and I'd definitely consider sampling some of his particular Tuscan hospitality, if it was on offer.

Besides, having dinner with Vico would spare me the awkwardness that was sure to manifest when I arrived at Fran's. In one sense, I would be early. But in the most meaningful way, I was far too late.

We drove on down the road, leaving a trail of dust behind us. In the fields beside us, the grasses undulated like waves in the ocean. I shot the occasional glance behind me to make sure the Diva wasn't about to fall over, but Vico had done a good job with the tie-downs.

The companionable silence suited my mood. No prying questions. No pressure to make small talk. Maybe we both had a lot on our minds.

The sun was just a golden glow on the horizon when

Vico turned into a long, winding drive lined with Tuscan cypress. Two or three kilometers away, the village of San Donato shone on the hillside, its stone buildings and tiled roofs warm and peaceful in the last rays of the sun.

Vico pulled up to an old stone cottage. Further up the drive, a large villa perched at the top of the hill, with several outbuildings scattered about. This looked like a substantial working farm, complete with a grove of olive trees and fields of some crop I couldn't immediately identify, botany not being my specialty. Vico hopped out of the truck.

He yelled into the door of the cottage. *"Nonna, ho portato un ospite per cena."*

A thin voice answered him from the bowels of the house. *"Che palle! Lo sai que odio le sorprese."*

"Dai, Nonna."

A wizened woman in an apron gripped the doorframe and gave me the once-over as I clambered out of the truck. *"Bah! Portala dentro. La cena è quasi pronta."* She waved a dismissive hand and disappeared back inside. The timeless odor of garlic and simmering tomatoes drifted out towards me.

"Are you sure this is OK?" I hadn't caught much of their exchange but Nonna hadn't seemed too happy to see me.

Vico grinned. His dimple gave me a slight heart palpitation. "She is always like this when I bring home a woman. No one is good enough for her Vico. Pay no attention."

"It's not like I'm marrying you."

"No, but she thinks every woman wants to. She will never change." He rolled his eyes, then gave me a sly smile. "Although it is disappointing that you dismiss me so quickly. We have only just met." He jerked his head at the door. "Come. Dinner waits."

"Just a second." I clambered up into the bed of the pickup, opened one of my saddlebags and took out the portable liner bag. I suspected it wasn't a good idea to sit down at Nonna's table in sweaty riding gear.

Then I followed Vico into the house, where my mouth immediately watered at the rich smells emanating from the kitchen. The cottage was typical Italian rustic, with stone and plaster walls, wood beam ceilings, and clay tile floors. Vico went into the kitchen to kiss his grandmother, who was bustling away at the stove. He retrieved an extra place setting and set it down on the table.

"Is there anywhere I can change?"

"Of course. Although you are more than fine like that." Vico's gaze drifted over my riding leathers, his eyes lingering a little longer than necessary. The gear *did* highlight my curves. Maybe we'd have to start a mutual admiration society. I'd have to up my flirting game if I wanted to catch up.

"Thank you. But I think I'd prefer something a little more breathable."

"Then follow me." He led me upstairs into a small bedroom towards the back of the cottage. He grabbed a clean shirt and jeans from a dresser. "I will go wash if you do not need water. The bathroom is next door."

"No, I'm fine."

He closed the door behind him. I shed my boots, wincing as I caught sight of my blisters. I shimmied out of the leathers and the T-shirt I'd been wearing, grabbed my deodorant and did my best to dust off and cover up the afternoon's road grime. Then I slipped into my all-occasion wrinkle-free travel skirt and a fresh V-necked top.

I undid the braid I kept my hair in while riding, combed it out with my fingers, and bent over, fluffing up my hair in a vain attempt to banish my helmet head. I examined myself in the mirror that hung next to the door. Not great, but it would have to do.

I grimaced as I tried to slide my feet into my flip-flops. I had a blister on my left heel and one on my right foot, just on the side behind my big toe. I padded out of the bedroom and listened at the bathroom door. Not hearing any running water, I knocked.

Vico opened up, still toweling off his hair. He was shirtless, his waist wrapped in another towel, drops of water glistening here and there on his tanned skin.

What Roman god had dropped this living Renaissance sculpture into my life? *You're closer to Siena, El.* Rome, Siena, tomayto-tomahto. Same gods, weren't they? Or maybe they were Etruscan here?

I resisted the temptation to run my hands across his chest. A part of me craved the simple, clean comfort of an uncomplicated hookup, but was this really the best time? I cleared my throat. "Do you have Bandaids?"

He gave me a puzzled look.

I lifted my foot a bit and pointed at my blister.

Vico made a face. *"Ai. Si. Cerotti. Un minuto."* He disappeared into the bathroom, closing the door, so I wandered back into the bedroom and sat on the bed. He reappeared—fully clothed, to my eternal disappointment, his hair still damp and tousled—with a box of bandages.

Instead of handing them to me, he knelt down, clasped my ankles and rested my feet on his thighs. As if it was the most natural thing in the world to tend to a complete stranger's feet. I found his lack of artifice endearing, and suppressed my usual control-freak tendencies. It was nice being taken care of for once.

He selected a plaster from the assortment in the box and deftly opened the wrapper. He applied the bandage to my heel, then repeated the process for the blister on the side of my other foot, smoothing the dressing out gently with his fingers, his grip on my skin firm so as not to tickle. He paused, my foot still in his hand, and cocked his head. "You have lovely feet."

Despite the sudden warmth running up my spine at his touch, I snickered. The skin on my feet was creased from my motorcycle socks and boots, red pressure marks and angry welts visible here and there.

"Why do you laugh?" Vico's hand drifted over the top of my foot, caressing my ankle. He looked up at me, his eyes a startling light grey against his tawny skin. "They are the feet of a woman with a well-lived life. *Particolare.*"

My breath hitched. His hand still rubbed lightly across my skin, warm and solid.

He didn't push, though, and ironically that lack of insistence kindled my interest. He looked at me not as a prize to snatch and display, but as someone to be savored.

And that was almost irresistible.

The moment hung in the balance, poised between flirting and something more.

"Vico! La cena è in tavola!"

Vico shook his head and, giving me a wry look, released my foot. He slapped his thighs, stood, and extended a hand to help me up from the bed. "Always perfect timing, *la nonna*. Come. Dinner awaits."

I followed him back to the dining room. I *was* hungry.

Just not for dinner.

CHAPTER TWO

NONNA ungently set a bowl in front of me, soup sloshing up
its sides. *"La zuppa."*

Vico brought two more bowls. "It is ribollita—bread
soup."

I set to with gusto. The tomato-based soup was chock-full
of vegetables and cannellini beans, with soaking chunks of
bread mixed in. "It's delicious."

Nonna watched me through slitted eyes as if she didn't
trust my appetite. She finished her smaller portion and
headed out to the kitchen again.

"Is this your farm?"

Vico laughed. "No. I manage it for the owner."

"And your grandmother?"

"She has lived here her whole life. The land used to be
our family's."

"What happened?"

"Life. Bad luck. Debts. My great-grandfather sold it long
before I was born."

"That must be hard, working land that isn't yours anymore."

Vico shrugged. *"Così è la vita."*

After my lunch, I'd have been happy just with the soup, but Vico grabbed my bowl when we were done and it was clear I was in for further courses. Nonna trundled back to the table and slapped a plate of ragu-covered gnocchi in front of me. Vico uncorked a bottle of Chianti and poured three glasses. *"Salute."*

I raised mine. *"Salute."* I looked at Nonna. *"Grazie per la cena."* Then to Vico. "And for the rescue."

"It was nothing."

Nonna gestured at our plates impatiently. *"Mangiate. Si sta raffreddando tutto."*

"Nonna is right. Food is better when it's hot."

The hot item I really wanted was sitting across the table from me, but I popped a dumpling into my mouth. It exploded and vanished on contact with my tongue. "Mmph!" My eyes widened in delight. I'd never had gnocchi so light and fluffy.

"You like?" Vico asked.

"Very much."

"Nonna braises the beef for hours."

I raised my wineglass to her. *"È buonissimo."* I might not be fluent but I'd acquired a smattering of Italian since starting the contract I'd taken in Varese.

Nonna gave me a look that told me exactly how little she valued my praise. I took Vico's advice and let it slide.

Anybody who made food this good wasn't going to get an argument from me.

"Dille che i gnocchi li hai fatti tu." Nonna glared at Vico.

"What did she say?"

Vico looked embarrassed. "She wants me to tell you I made the gnocchi." He gave Nonna an even look. *"È la tua ricetta."*

"Bah!" Nonna made grumpy noises but this time a small smile curled up the corners of her mouth.

"You made the gnocchi?"

"The dumplings, not the sauce. I … like to cook. Nonna taught me. If the gnocchi are good, it is because of her."

"Well, they really are superb." A man who cooked. Be still my famished heart. And one who seemed more concerned with making sure his grandmother got all the credit. Refreshing, considering why I'd left Montréal. I raised my glass to Nonna. "You taught him well."

Nonna grunted and tucked into her food. For a while I didn't feel the need to make conversation as I simply enjoyed the meal. Nonna and Vico chattered away in rapid-fire Italian, while I caught every third word. I guessed they were discussing something relating to Vico's deliveries today. I was just happy listening to the musical flow of their words. I loved letting language wash over me, even if I didn't understand.

Their animated conversation and the fantastic food conjured up a cocoon of warmth and contentment. It felt good to be welcomed somewhere, after the last few months of trying to fit into a new city, new country, new job, new life, all while knowing it was probably temporary. Vico and Nonna were a family. Something I hadn't had in a while. Something I had even less of now.

Vico looked at me. "You are very quiet, Elodia."

I gave myself a little shake. It wasn't polite to mourn at the dinner table. "It was a long day of riding. A little stressful there at the end."

"But all is fine now, no?"

I smiled. "Everything is more than fine. Thanks to you and Nonna's kindness."

Nonna got up and cleared the plates.

"Can I help with the dishes, at least?" This old lady and her grandson had just fed me the most amazing home-cooked food, and I didn't want to seem ungrateful.

Nonna gestured peremptorily.

OK then. Sit down it is.

Vico smiled. "I am the only other person Nonna allows in the kitchen. Come, she will be happier if we sit outside and leave her alone." He grabbed the wine bottle and I followed him to a small patio outside, overlooking the valley. We sank down into adjoining lounge chairs.

"It is your first time in Tuscany?"

"Yes. I meant to visit sooner but work got in the way." And now I'd always have that regret.

"Are you staying long?"

"I need to be in the area for at least a week, I think"— between the funeral and the lawyers I doubted I'd be back at work before that—"but I'm hoping there's time to explore in there somewhere. I'd like to see Siena."

"Volterra and San Gimignano are very pretty also."

"So I've heard."

Lights glowed in the valley below us, and the stars spread out in a wide canopy overhead.

"Buona notte, Vico!" Nonna's voice echoed from inside the house.

"Sogni d'oro, Nonna!" Vico called back. "Nonna is going to bed."

"Is she now?"

He tilted the bottle to refill my glass, stopped just before pouring "Do you need to go to bed also?"

"I guess it depends on the bed."

Vico's eyes glittered in the starlight. He poured the wine.

I decided to lay my cards on the table. I'd met a number of Italian men since I'd landed, many of them handsome and accomplished, many of them interested in me, but none who had piqued my interest quite like Vico. Most of them had been colleagues, due to the nature of my job. I'd turned down several offers of drinks with my peers, especially after one admitted there was a minor office betting pool going as to who would bed me first. I just wanted to do my job, dammit.

But that didn't mean I wanted to be a nun, or that I wasn't lonely. Vico … Vico had shown his interest in no uncertain terms, but done so with an understated charm I found seductive. With the transfer, and the work, I'd been a little too busy to meet many men outside the office, especially since I was trying to avoid the kind of complications a work relationship might entail. But why resist now? I had some time to myself for the first time since arriving in Italy, and Vico … well, Vico was a morsel too tasty to pass up.

He was sexy. And considerate. And kind.

And I could use some good old-fashioned comfort, of the physical sort. It had been a hard few months, and an even harder few days. I needed the solace and the warmth of another human being. Vico was welcoming me with open arms. What better way to take my mind off death for a while than the ultimate celebration of life?

I took a sip of wine. "Do you know what women who ride motorcycles find sexy?"

Vico shook his head.

"Men who cook."

"Ah." He reached out, ran a finger along my forearm. "Do you know what men who cook find sexy?"

"Tell me."

"Women who ride motorcycles."

"What a happy coincidence."

"What do you think it means?"

"That you should stop talking and kiss me."

He leaned across the armrests, cupped my nape, and pressed his mouth to mine. I parted my lips and let him taste me, savored his earthy flavor in return as his tongue explored my mouth. He leaned back, his eyes hooded and sensuous, patted his lap. *"Vieni qui."*

I climbed out of my chair and onto his, settled into his

lap, kissed him again. The crickets sang in the tall grass as we necked.

I clasped his face between my hands, his stubble prickly against my palms. His arms circled me, one hand at the small of my back, the other scrubbing through my hair, cupping the back of my head. I sank into his embrace. I lapped at his tongue, drawing out the kiss, luxuriating in the heat of our joined mouths, my desire for him and his for me.

This felt right, and some of the tension I'd been hoarding left my body. All my doubts about fitting into my new life vanished in the sudden certainty that right now, this was exactly where I belonged. I drifted my fingers along Vico's jaw and the side of his throat, the other hand tangling in his silky hair. He smelled of lemon soap, clean and crisp.

His hand slipped beneath my T-shirt, caressing my back, the calluses on his palms scraping lightly against my skin. I pressed myself closer against his chest, seeking out the warmth of his body as a buffer against the cool night breeze.

I could have kissed him like this forever, but his hand trailed down my back, stroked along the curve of my ass and the side of my thigh, stretching the smooth fabric of my skirt until he reached the hem and found skin near my knee. He slid his fingers beneath my skirt, palming my thigh just above the knee.

He paused. "Do you want me to stop, *tesoro?*" His lips played against mine as he spoke.

I gave his question the consideration it deserved, and stoppered his mouth with my tongue. I'd made my decision when he first asked me about bed, and now that I'd felt his confident, enthusiastic touch, I had absolutely no reason to change my mind. Vico was the joyful chaser to a not-so-great couple of days, and the high from this little romp might even gird me for the week to come. A little consequence-free fun was just what I needed.

Besides, he tasted too good.

I drew deeply on his tongue, and he made a soft noise in the back of his throat, surrendering briefly before mounting his own offensive. His hand squeezed my thigh, then climbed, until he pressed the heel of his palm low against my mound, his fingers splayed across my belly, stroking, petting, teasing against the elastic of my underwear. I pushed against his hand, let him feel the heat of me. My head dropped back and he kissed my throat.

I let out a small sigh as he eased his fingers beneath the waistband of my panties, then down, into the softest part of me, teasing apart my folds. He dipped into me, slowly, rubbing and slicking as I squirmed against him, massaging until I started to pant. His thumb circled my clit and I circled my hips with it. As I found my own rhythm, he stiffened his fingers and thumb, letting me pleasure myself at my own pace.

"*È giusto, tesoro,*" he murmured.

He cradled my head and shoulders and as I arched back, fucking myself against his hand, he whispered soft Italian endearments into my ear until finally I gasped and clenched against his fingers, stifling my cry of release so as not to wake

Nonna.

He feathered soft kisses along my jawline. I shifted my weight, wriggling upright until I could plant a kiss on his forehead. My core pulsed and ticked like a cooling engine.

"Perhaps now it is time for bed," Vico said, "unless you are expected somewhere. I can still drive you." He stroked his hand against my flank and the hard bulge digging into my hip told me just how disappointed he'd be if I said I had to go. *I'd be disappointed if I left now.*

"It's pretty late, and Aunt Fran's people aren't expecting me until tomorrow. Maybe if I'd shown up at dinnertime, but now I might wake them."

He recoiled, his arms stiffening against me. "Wait. Your 'Aunt Fran?' You are Francesca Leduc's niece?"

"Grand-niece. How did you know?"

"*Cazzo.*" He sat up, nearly dumping me from his lap.

I got up from my now precarious perch. What had just happened? "Vico—"

"*Mi dispiace*, but I must take you home now." He stood, shifting his hips slightly in discomfort, then stalked into the house.

I gaped at the space he'd just been in, the feeling of his hands on and in me fresh and raw. By the time I caught up with him, he was standing at the cottage's front door with my saddle liner bag in one hand and my riding gear draped over the other arm. He nodded at my boots. "You will have to carry those. Come." He disappeared out the door, leaving me no choice but to follow.

He headed for the truck.

"Vico, please talk to me. What is going on?"

Instead of getting in, Vico passed the truck and started up the driveway. To the large villa on the hill. I might be slow, but not that slow. Dawning realization hit me, but I needed to hear it from him. "Vico, where are you taking me?"

"Home."

"My aunt's place is called Fiera Vista di Cortine." I was a little out of breath from the steepness of the drive. My flip-flops were almost as bad as my riding boots at handling gravel surfaces.

"Yes, I know." He nodded at the villa. "You have arrived."

"Vico—"

He turned, finally letting me catch up. Two Tuscan cypresses towered to either side of us, dark sentinels against the stars. "Allow me to welcome you. I am Lodovico Fierli. I am the caretaker of your aunt's estate. *Le mie più profonde condoglianze* ... my sympathies to you at her passing."

Well, damn. Wasn't that the juiciest cherry on top of the cake El can't have and eat too. I'd gotten off, but definitely not on the right foot. I sighed and trudged up the drive after Vico.

Awkward didn't begin to cover this.

CHAPTER THREE

I tossed a clod of earth into the hole where Fran's coffin lay.
The priest droned on in solemn Italian. Across from me,
Vico and Nonna stood with hands clasped. Other mourners
from the village and Fran's substantial group of friends
clustered about the grave.

As Francesca Leduc's only living relative, I felt
significantly out of place among her contemporaries. They'd
all known her better than I had.

Oh sure, there'd been the usual birthday cards and
Christmas gifts, but given the geographical and generational
distance between us, Fran was the kind of relative one only
thought about from time to time. I'd written to her when I'd
received the job transfer, suggesting a visit—as my father's
mother's sister she'd always been the mysterious black sheep
in the family, moving from Montréal at a young age to marry
her playboy sweetheart, and I was curious to finally meet her.

She'd sent back an enthusiastic reply, inviting me to stay
later in the summer, as my new role didn't permit me much

initial downtime, and the four-hour drive to Cortine from Varese in northern Italy didn't fit nicely into a weekend getaway even when I wasn't dawdling on backroads taking in the countryside. That trip had been on my calendar for four weeks from now.

And then the letter from her executor had arrived, and I'd suddenly had to come to terms with the fact that I was now completely alone in the world.

The if-onlys piled up around my feet like the dirt piling onto Fran's coffin. If only I'd visited sooner. If only the Diva hadn't broken down. If only I hadn't thrown myself at Vico.

Because if I thought my prospective welcome as Fran's last, long-lost distant relative was dicey before, what must Vico think of me now? Dad had implied there was a scandal in Fran's long-ago elopement—though he'd never elaborated —and here I came, living up to the family reputation.

I sighed.

The priest finished talking, and Nonna crossed herself. Fran's friends drifted over to shake my hand and offer their sympathies, and then cars started up as people set out for the wake I was hosting at the villa. Or rather, that Vico was hosting. Vico nodded towards the car and I trailed after him and Nonna to the parking lot.

As the Diva still wouldn't start, and showing up to a funeral in my leathers would have raised a few eyebrows anyway, I'd come with Vico and Nonna in their car. There'd been no time to have Vico drive me to Florence or Siena to pick up a rental.

Nonna's strange sense of honor wouldn't let a guest sit anywhere but in the front seat, so despite my protests she crammed her aged frame into the back while I sat beside Vico.

I stared out the window as we drove back to Fran's villa, trying to focus on putting my hostess face on for our guests, but all I could think about was Vico next to me. His lips set in a grim line instead of curved in satisfaction at my pleasure. His hand on the gear shift instead of my knee.

I shook my head. That first night …

That first night, Vico had unlocked the door to the villa, flicked on the lights, and led me to a guest room on the second floor. Any sense of intimacy between us had vanished, his friendly flirting replaced with an all-business politeness.

He deposited my gear on the quilted bedspread. "The bathroom is across the hall. There is food in the kitchen but Nonna can fix you breakfast if you like."

"No, I'll be fine, thank you."

"Is there anything else you need?"

Aside from a cold shower? "No."

Vico handed me a set of keys. "For the house, while you stay." He walked past me, paused in the doorway. "Your aunt was a lovely woman. We grieve her death deeply. She contributed much to the village. My deepest sympathies to you."

And with that, he was gone, his feet clacking on the stairs. The main entrance door clunked shut behind him. The silence of an empty house pooled around me.

I opened the shutters on my window to air out the room, which was slightly stuffy. The armoire contained a white cotton bathrobe, which I purloined before heading to the bathroom to shed my damp underwear and take that shower.

I spent the rest of the night staring at the room's timbered ceiling, unable to sleep for hours, until just before dawn I drifted off, dreaming of Vico's lips against my cheek, his warm arms wrapped around me.

He'd disappeared the next day, giving me no opportunity to set things right between us. Nonna, muttering imprecations, had shooed me away from the cottage, from which the most amazing smells continued to emanate. Had he told her what happened?

And now here I was, trying desperately not to think inappropriate thoughts about him on a day when I should only be thinking about Aunt Fran.

Ironic that in trying to obtain a brief sense of belonging I'd shot my best chance at a deeper one in the foot.

Vico pulled up to the front door and we all made our way into the house. Nonna beelined straight for the kitchen, while Vico stayed by the door to greet new arrivals.

The house teemed with conversation, a far cry from the quietness that had filled it for the past day and a half. Friends of Fran and other mourners clustered in small groups in the large formal living and dining room. The triple set of doors to the patio had been flung open, and people stood out in the sun by Fran's enormous pool.

Vico had enlisted catering staff to help serve the abundance of food laid out on the dining room table. I accepted a glass of Chianti from a young woman and tried not to look too out of place in Fran's chi-chi house, a far cry from my middle-class roots.

Fran's estate lawyer and executor, Signore Galanti, approached in the company of a tall, silver-haired gentleman, perhaps of the age my father would have been. "Signorina Martel, may I present Signore Gianni Mirri, a great friend of your aunt's."

Mirri took my hand, pressing it to his lips. Was that his tongue? Ew. "My deepest sympathies."

I'd have believed him more if he hadn't just done something so squicky. But I was here for Aunt Fran. I snatched my hand back. "And to you, sir. You probably knew Fran better than I did."

"She was very much looking forward to the visit you'd planned later this summer. She spoke highly of your father— her favorite nephew, she always said."

He'd been her only nephew, but tact might be the better part of valor in this case. "Dad would have been happy to hear that."

"Yes, Francesca was saddened to hear of his passing."

I gave Mirri a wan smile. "I guess we're all saddened these days."

Mirri changed the subject. "What brought you to Italy?"

"My company sent me on a temporary transfer to Varese." Not the whole truth, but enough for polite company.

"Doing what?"

"I'm an aerospace engineer. I design plane engines. There's a plant just on the outskirts of Varese that does work for Airbus."

"How very … nontraditional."

I repressed a side-eye and my kneejerk "Only if your traditions are outdated" retort. I was used to men of a certain age raising sceptical eyebrows at my profession. "Chances are, if you've flown on a plane that's newer than five years old, my work is keeping you safe and airborne."

Mirri nudged Galanti. "Perhaps we need to stop flying."

Wow. Not even trying to hide the condescension now. Mirri went from dirty old fart to active dislike in my personal relationship ledger. I gritted my teeth, and left my reply at "Your loss." This was my aunt's funeral, after all, and I wasn't here to cause a scene.

I must not have been able to completely suppress the displeasure from my expression, because Mirri leaned over to pat my arm. "I was only joking, my dear."

Mmm-hmmm. And my engines are great at keeping pigs in the sky too. I changed the subject. "How did you meet my aunt?"

"Through mutual friends in Firenze. We were something of an item." Really? Fran with a boy toy? I wasn't sure what to make of her taste in men. "I would visit her here often, although I always thought she could do more with the place."

"How so?"

"It is perfectly situated to capitalize on Tuscan tourism. Just look at that view." Through the windows, the rolling hills of Tuscany, patterned with farms, vineyards, and tiny villages did their best to prove his point.

Still, my aunt had been quite elderly. I couldn't see her wanting to run a B&B in her dotage. "I guess the new owner will have that option."

Mirri gave me an unctuous smile. "Yes, they certainly will."

"If you'll excuse me, I have to check on the other guests." I beat a hasty retreat. Gianni Mirri gave me the urge to take a shower. My aunt was barely in the ground and he was sizing up her estate. I made a note to find out if Galanti knew any more about this man's intentions. We were supposed to go over Fran's will together tomorrow. She'd been a philanthropist for most of her life, and her charitable trust stood to benefit enormously from her death.

I wandered over to the buffet, admiring the mouth-watering spread. Pecorino cheese with prosciutto and other cured meats and sausages, crostini with liver paté, antipasti, and tomatoes everywhere—in pappa al pomodoro, another traditional bread soup; in panzanella, a light summer salad, again with bread; on bruschetta; in the sauces of the heaping bowls of primi. Grilled vegetables abounded, and I even spotted some fried zucchini flowers, which I made a note to try.

A lightbulb went on in my head as I heaped food onto my plate, and I snuck over to the kitchen and peeked in the door. At the center of the bustling catering staff, Nonna stood ladling a rich meat sauce over papardelle noodles.

I shut the door before she spotted me. She had *not* made all this food. It was unreasonable to ask a woman her age to cater an event like this. But I hadn't seen the caterers arrive this morning with any actual food, just stemware, plates, and cutlery. Nonna must have been working nonstop for the past twenty-four hours, maybe longer.

That *would* explain how amazing the cottage had smelled yesterday.

By the time I located Vico, I'd worked myself into a proper huff about it.

"Vico, can I talk to you?"

Vico smiled politely at a woman walking by. "We are talking, *si?*"

"In private?"

"Now?" Vico sighed. "*Va bene.* Follow me." He led me across the patio and into Fran's pool house, which was more like a private guest suite. The hubbub of conversation muted as he shut the door behind us. He kept an acquaintance-appropriate distance between us, which let me admire how good he looked in a suit, if not satisfy my deep craving to touch him. "The other night—"

"This isn't about the other night." Although I was tempted to make it so.

"It is not?"

"No. It's about Nonna."

Vico frowned. "What has she said now? I told her not to bother you."

"Vico, she's not bothering me. But the woman's not

superhuman. I'm sure Aunt Fran's estate provisioned enough money for proper catering so that Nonna didn't have to slave in the kitchen for who knows how long making all this food."

Vico did a spit-take. "Nonna didn't make the food."

"Then what's she doing in the kitchen? The wait staff certainly didn't make it. They didn't come in a big enough truck."

"*Ai*. She doesn't feel comfortable among your aunt's friends. She must have gone to hide in the kitchen."

"She's doing more than hiding. And you didn't answer my question. Who made the food?"

Vico shook his head as if he'd rather not be in this conversation. "I did."

I gaped at him. "You made *all* that food?"

"Why does it matter?"

"I—" I stopped talking, rethought my next words. I was in danger of offending him in exactly the same manner Signore Mirri had offended me. "I thought you were the estate caretaker, not a chef."

"I am both. I have a Masters in Italian Cuisine from the Apicius school in Firenze."

"You certainly do." Because that food was delicious. "Why aren't you working in some high-end restaurant in Florence?"

"Nonna needs me. And Francesca—*scusatemi*, Signora Leduc—needed someone to manage Fiera Vista. It had become too much for her alone."

"Wouldn't it have been easier to just ask the caterers to do it all?"

"*Sì*. But I wanted to do this last thing for your aunt. She always said she loved my cooking."

I swallowed the sudden lump in my throat, blinked hard a few times. What a lovely gesture. He must have slaved away for days on that banquet.

I really *liked* Vico. I wished he hadn't retreated so precipitously as soon as he found out I was related to his boss. Why *had* he, anyway? It wasn't like Fran and I were close. But Vico was definitely jumpy and uncomfortable around me now, and I'd give anything to fix it. The timing of our little tryst was certainly awkward, but that didn't make us monsters.

"Vico, if she loved your food half as much as I do, then she really loved your food." Maybe I had an opening here. We could clear the air between us at a less fraught time, and in privacy. "Would you cook me dinner sometime?"

"Signorina Martel—"

"Vico, please. It's El. Especially after—"

"Elodia—" I loved the way he said it, Eh-LOW-dee-ah, instead of EH-luh-dee like everyone else, the long vowel on the O so lush and sexy on his tongue. "What happened the night we met will not happen again."

I stepped up to him, put my hand on his cheek, and caressed his hair, but he shied away. "That's a damn shame. May I ask why?" This close to him, that wonderful lemon soap scent tantalized my nostrils again. The proximity of his body and the brief touch I'd had of his skin set the sense memory in my nerve endings tingling. The warmth of unfulfilled longing spread through me.

And unless I was a very bad reader of people, Vico's body remembered too. He shifted slightly, his nostrils ever so slightly flared, his lips just parted, his breathing a little fast. I raised my hand again, irresistibly drawn to touch him, but he caught my wrist, his grip gentle but firm. "Elodia, *per favore*. I cannot. Nonna would not like it."

Nonna? What the hell. I'd found the ultimate momma's boy. "What does Nonna have to do with anything?"

Vico scrubbed a hand through his hair. "*Perbacco*. Nothing. And everything. I *cannot*, Elodia."

I sighed, moved aside so he could leave. "Fine. If that's the way it has to be, I'll respect your wishes. But I'd still love that dinner, if that's OK with Nonna."

Vico hesitated.

I pulled out the big guns. "Would you have cooked Fran and I dinner if she'd been alive when I visited later this summer?"

"*Sì.*"

"Then I rest my case. Besides, who better to tell me all the great stories I never heard about my aunt than one of the people who knew her best? I didn't get to meet her, but maybe through you I can get a better sense of her." I gave him my best "I dare you to contradict me" smile.

"*Ai.* Fine. Tomorrow night."

"Perfect. I'll be seeing Signore Galanti in the afternoon. It's a date."

"It's not a date."

I rolled my eyes. "You know what I mean."

"That is what I am afraid of."

Maybe I wasn't being as coy as I thought.

CHAPTER FOUR

"I'M sorry, Signore Galanti, but I don't understand."

"What is to understand, Signorina Martel? With the exception of the provision for Signora Fierli and her grandson, your aunt named you as her sole heir."

"But we'd never even met."

"Signora Leduc believed firmly in family."

Given her absence from ours, I'd never have guessed. "What about her charitable trust?"

"That has become self-sustaining over the years. I recommend keeping the current administrator."

I got up, stretched a kink out of my neck, and paced the room, trying to release some of the nervous energy Signore Galanti's news had brought.

"Forgive me, Signorina Martel, but you do not look very happy for someone who is now rich."

I put my hands on the back of the plush leather chair I'd just vacated. "Don't get me wrong, Signore Galanti. I'm very … pleased. It's just so unexpected." And what the hell was I going to do with a huge Tuscan estate? I was a mid-career engineer. I lived comfortably off my income, and had no debt to speak of. Aside from the recent unpleasantness back home that had brought about my transfer, I liked my life. What if this windfall changed it? You always heard about lottery winners coming into money and then imploding under the unfamiliarity of it all. "I just … I need some time to adjust, is all."

Signore Galanti rose as well. "Take all the time you need. There is some paperwork to sign for the accounts and property transfer, and the taxes will need to be paid. But we can deal with that when you are ready."

"*Grazie*, Signore Galanti."

"It is my pleasure, signorina. Your aunt was a delightful woman with whom I had a long and fruitful business relationship. I hope you will consider retaining my services should you need any help navigating the Italian legal system in the future."

I shook his hand, arranged a time to follow up with him, and tucked the envelope of paperwork he gave me under my arm. When I exited the office, I found Vico and Nonna sitting in Signore Galanti's waiting room. I was glad the lawyer had some good news for them. In the flurry of preparations for the funeral, I hadn't even considered that they might be under some stress, given the unknown ramifications of the passing of their landlord and employer.

I paused, waylaid Vico with a hand on his arm as he ushered Nonna into Galanti's office. "We're still on for dinner tonight, yes?"

"*Sì,* signorina. I honor my commitments."

I sighed. Still so formal. *Just take the win, El.* "Great. I'll see you later." I made my way back to Aunt Fran's vintage Mercedes, the keys to which Vico had found for me this morning. I dropped the sheaf of papers on the passenger seat and drove back to Fiera Vista lost in thought.

Work was expecting me back in a few days, but I suspected I might have to extend my leave. This was no longer just a pay my respects and swan off into the sunset kind of trip. Arriving at the house, I went out to Fran's—no, my patio, found a shady spot beneath the vine-draped pergola, and spread out the paperwork Galanti had given me.

It was a summary of Fran's accounts and assets. If I was adding up the numbers right, Fran had upwards of five million euros in investments, plus a substantial art collection whose assessed value topped two million. Then there was the estate, valued somewhere north of 1.5 million euros. Galanti hadn't been kidding: I was rich. The kind of rich I could quit my job and retire on.

The will specified that Nonna and Vico be allowed to stay on in the cottage until Nonna's death. There was a covenant on the property to prevent their eviction in the event of a sale or change in ownership, which complicated things for me if I ever did decide to list it.

At the bottom of the pile of papers, I found an envelope with my name scrawled in elegant handwriting, in the green ink that Fran had favored.

Dear Élodie,

It is one of my deep regrets in life that my journey and yours did not intersect. Please know that I followed your exploits and successes with interest whenever your father cared to write me.

It is my hope that though my bequest may come as a surprise, it offers you the freedom to pursue your interests as I have had the good fortune to pursue mine.

Do with it what you will, but please take care of Nonna. Should you care to keep Vico in your employ as the estate manager, I am sure he would appreciate the opportunity to remain close to his grandmother.

All my love,

Fran

I set down the letter and tried to fathom how my life had just changed, thanks to the generous whim of a woman I'd never met.

All I really knew of Fran was her taste in books—her preferred gift to me as I was growing up. She'd liked to send me the memoirs of accomplished women, travel diaries, biographies, and stories of female inventors and scientists. Tucked into each book would be a postcard from one of her own travels, always written in her signature green ink.

She never forgot a birthday or Christmas, even though I sometimes forgot to send a thank you card.

I remembered Dad telling me that she'd defrayed a major portion of Mom's funeral expenses after her long illness.

Fran hadn't been part of our lives, but she hadn't been absent, either. I thought about how all those books shaped me, perhaps even led me into my career and sowed the seeds for my willingness to start over in a new country.

She'd been the last one standing from her branch of the family, and now she'd passed the torch to me. I wondered if she'd felt a little like I did, all alone, or if she'd died content. She'd certainly lived her life on her own terms.

I regretted even more not being able to come visit from Varese before she'd died.

It was odd trying to mourn someone I didn't truly know. But even if I didn't feel a rending grief, the quiet sadness filling me now seemed appropriate.

Also the gratitude. Fran's strong allegiance to family had suddenly opened up frontiers to me I hadn't even contemplated before. "Thank you, Fran," I murmured.

Inside the house, the phone rang.

I trotted in to pick it up.

"Elodia?" Vico's voice sounded in the earpiece.

"Yes?"

"I cannot come for dinner."

In the background, Nonna was yelling. *Ti sei preso cura di lei per anni. Per anni!"*

Vico continued. "Nonna is very upset."

"I … see." What did Nonna have to be upset about? Signore Galanti must have told them about Fran's will, and assured them that nothing would change for them. "That's a shame. I guess I'll have to fend for myself, then." I tried to put a smile in my voice. "If I poison myself, it'll be your fault."

"Poison?"

"My cooking skills are that bad."

"Ah."

Nonna's tinny voice groused in a stream of rapid Italian invective.

"It's OK, Vico—"

Vico sighed. "No, it is not OK. Let me deal with Nonna, calm her. We will just eat later. Is this fine?"

"Sure. It'll just give the wine more time to breathe. Come up whenever."

"*Va bene.* See you later."

"I look forward to it. But Vico, I was only joking. If it's really going to cause you a problem—"

"No, no. I will come. *Ciao.*"

Just before the line went dead, Nonna's voice came through loud and clear. "*Quella puttana—*"

Oh dear. I understood that one even with my limited Italian. Was that directed at me?

If for whatever reason Nonna was that angry, maybe I wouldn't see Vico after all.

CHAPTER FIVE

WHILE I waited for Vico I uncorked a bottle of white wine, poured myself a glass, and took a stroll around the villa. Between Fran's funeral, the meeting with Signore Galanti, and various and sundry interruptions from grieving acquaintances of Fran, I hadn't had much time to explore the house or its surroundings. And since it was now my house, it was probably wise to get to know it a bit better.

The villa itself was an extensively renovated 11th-century building set high on a hill overlooking the Tuscan countryside, one of those ancient stone structures that had weathered the test of history and exuded serenity and timelessness. The exterior consisted of bare stone walls, clay-tiled roof, shuttered windows, and a large patio next to a turquoise pool. An exterior staircase climbed to the second floor. The facade had an unfussy lack of ornamentation, relying on its simple lines for its understated elegance. Bouffant lavender and sage bushes delineated the patio area, and a large garden surrounded most of the house, before giving way to agricultural land.

Further down the hill stood several outbuildings for the farm equipment and livestock—Fiera Vista was a working farm, with fields of barley and durum wheat, an olive grove, and small vineyard. According to Signore Galanti's documents, the farm earned some revenue selling its produce locally, but was mostly in the red.

Inside, the main floor consisted of a large open-plan living/dining area with an array of French doors opening to the patio. At the far end of the entertaining space, a massive fireplace squatted against the wall. The walls were a pale plaster, the floors all tile. Fran had left the ceiling beams exposed, with the second floor's planks visible above.

A modern chef's kitchen sat just off the dining room, with a huge pantry and stairs leading down to a root cellar. When I ventured into its cool depths, I found shelves stacked with maturing cheeses and cured meats, a veritable wonderland of Tuscan epicurean bounty. My stomach rumbled.

On my way out of the kitchen, I refilled my wine glass and explored some more. Towards the front of the house, I found a library and study, and beyond that, Fran's master bedroom and ensuite, which made sense since at her age the stairs to the second floor might have proven problematic. Up those stairs were a further five bedrooms and their associated amenities.

I frowned. For someone who supposedly had a lot of art, none of it was hanging on the walls. Maybe she kept it hidden away in a secure spot somewhere? I came from the school of thought that said art should be enjoyed, not socked away as an investment, but Fran grew up in a different world. Maybe it was just an investment to her.

What would I do rattling around a place this size by myself? What had Fran done?

As I made my way downstairs and back to the patio, a small lizard scuttled across the tiles. I guess I wasn't that alone.

I spread out the papers on the table and studied them further, at least the ones that weren't written in Italian. The monthly outlays for upkeep on Fiera Vista were eye-opening. I would need to talk to Signore Galanti about just how liquid Fran's investments were, because my own salary, while decent, sure wouldn't cover the costs of maintenance and Vico's salary, nor underwrite the seasonal workers for the farm. The bills would rack up quickly, and if I wasn't careful, Fiera Vista had the potential to quickly turn into an albatross.

My contract in Varese was only temporary, and if I moved back to Montréal afterwards, what did that mean for Fiera Vista? Could I keep an eye on an estate this size remotely?

I also made a note to get an updated investment statement balance, because the one Galanti had provided was over a year old.

Something clanged in the kitchen. I swept up the papers, stuffed them back into their envelope, and went in to see if Vico had in fact arrived or if one of the Tuscan lizards had

had a misadventure.

Vico looked up as I entered the kitchen. "Are you allergic to seafood?"

"No."

"Then that will be the theme tonight."

"May I watch?"

"You will work." He jutted his chin out slightly, indicating some green onions on the counter. "Chop, *per favore*."

I slid a knife out of one of Fran's knife blocks and set to on the onions while Vico peeled garlic.

"*Così lenta!* Who taught you how to use a knife?"

"Nobody, really."

"It is a mother's first duty, showing her daughter the kitchen."

I sighed. "My mother died before she could pass along her skills. Dad was too busy working to show me around a kitchen." Dinners at our place had often consisted of take-out, or grilled meat on the barbecue.

"*Mi dispiace*, Elodia. I did not realize."

I shrugged. "It was a long time ago. I figured things out on my own when I got bored with microwaved meals."

Vico grimaced. "Don't let Nonna hear you talk about the microwave. She calls it the instrument of the devil." He brandished his knife. "Watch. I will turn you into a sous-chef yet." He showed me how to hold the food so I wouldn't slice off my fingertips, then chopped a stalk of the onion in a motion so fast his hand almost blurred.

"Whoa."

"Now you try."

I awkwardly imitated his grip and attempted to reproduce his motion, but succeeded mostly in slicing air.

"You must push the food along too."

"I get that, but it's easier said than done."

"Here, you are holding the knife wrong." He sidled closer, closed his hand around mine and repositioned my fingers. "You see? Like this." Our joined hands made a cutting motion. "Do not try for speed at first. First coordination. Then faster." He tilted his head, gave me a sly glance. "You did not lie about your abilities in the kitchen."

"I'm nothing if not honest, Vico."

"Yes. It's what I like about you."

I were being truly honest, I might have mentioned how nice his grip felt on my hand. He was so close I could have leaned over and kissed him. I decided to tease instead. He'd been clear about his ground rules and I should respect them. That didn't mean I wasn't curious, though. "So you still like me, then?"

Vico sighed and edged away. "Liking you is not the problem, Elodia."

"You said Nonna is."

Seeing I was nearly done with the onions, Vico slid a red pepper across the counter to me, then he went to the fridge, took out some prawns, and started peeling them. He frowned the whole time, and I sensed he was debating how much to say. "You know what julienning is?"

I nodded, and started working on the peppers.

"Nonna's father used to own this land. After the war, times were hard. The family had already moved to the cottage because the villa was too big. A rich man from the city offered to buy the estate. He said he was in love with Nonna, that their marriage would keep the land in the family. So my great-grandfather agreed to the sale. The buyer was not a farmer and needed workers, so my great-grandfather hoped his grandsons would work the land as he had."

"What happened?"

"The rich man went abroad. And he met Francesca."

I stopped chopping. "Oh." This was the scandal Dad had never explained. Ancient history, he'd said. But some of that history still lived here.

"Yes. *Oh.*" Vico took a large swig of wine from the glass he'd poured himself, and arched a wry eyebrow at me. "Nonna never forgave Francesca."

Fran's husband sounded like the real villain here but I let that go. "And Nonna's stayed here the whole time anyway?"

Vico put some butter in a skillet to melt, then started shredding marinated artichoke he retrieved from a jar. "There wasn't much good work at the time, so Nonna's father stayed on to tend the farm. Nonna eventually married and in time her husband took over management of the estate. Then my father after him."

Continuing the family tradition. Even though they didn't own the land. Twisted. "But you went to chef school."

"Yes." Vico tossed the garlic and onions into the pan, squeezed in some lemon juice, then seared the prawns.

I watched him cooking, his strong farmer's hands gripping the handle of the skillet. The agile motion of his wrists as he tossed the prawns. His quiet efficiency as he prepped a bed of the shredded artichoke on two plates then topped it with the prawns. He was spending the best years of his life taking care of two little old ladies. "You don't want to farm. You'd rather be doing this."

Vico shrugged, brought the plates to the kitchen island, and sat down on one of the bar stools there. I took the hint and joined him. Vico handed me a fork. "After my own parents died, there was no one to care for Nonna. She is too old to live alone, and she refuses to move. She says she will die on this land, and who am I to tell her no? This is not a bad life for me." He gestured at my plate with his fork. "You like?"

I took a bite of the appetizer to mask my discomfiture, nodded as the fresh summer flavors spread across my tongue. Vico told a fine story, but I sensed there was more. "I still don't get it, though. Why was Nonna so upset by what Signore Galanti had to say? She gets to stay. Isn't that what she wants?"

Vico kept his eyes downcast, refusing to meet my gaze. "What makes you think it was about the will?"

"Come on, Vico. My Italian's not great but she was shouting about some woman earlier. Did she get some other news today besides the will?"

Vico shook his head.

"Then the logical conclusion is she meant me or Fran."

"We Italians aren't known as the most logical of people."

"Vico."

His shoulders slumped. "Several years ago, Francesca led Nonna to believe that she would leave the estate to me."

I nearly dropped my fork.

Vico's mouth turned down. "So today … came as an unpleasant surprise."

I'd come as an unpleasant surprise. Shit.

CHAPTER SIX

I finished my plate in silence, Vico's delicious food like cardboard in my mouth. I'd wanted to hear stories about Fran, but hadn't bargained on this. When Vico set his fork down I picked up both plates and carried them to the sink. He got up to toss pasta in the pot of water he'd set to boil before we sat down. I leaned my hands on the edge of the sink, watching Vico out of the corner of my eye.

He was still making me dinner. After I'd blithely shown up out of nowhere and usurped what he and Nonna saw as rightfully theirs. Nonna had just watched a second person from my family dash her hopes and dreams. No wonder she was so pissed.

"Vico …"

He looked up from the skillet where he was now sautéing the peppers and some squid. There was absolutely no bitterness in the clear grey eyes peering at me from beneath his fluffy dark bangs.

"I didn't know. I'm so sorry. You don't need to do this."

"Do what?"

"This." I waved my arms to encompass the kitchen. "Cooking me dinner. Spending the evening with the last person you want to be with tonight." It was too much to bear.

He stared down at the stove, a small sad smile wilting at the corners of his lips. "Ah, but Elodia … what makes you think you are such a person?"

I faced him fully. "Am I not?" He hadn't exactly been enthusiastic about my company lately, and now I understood much better why.

"Nonna is the angry one. I cannot blame you for Francesca's choices."

"But being here is coming between you and Nonna. I don't want to be responsible for that."

"All signs to the contrary, Nonna does not rule my life. Besides, cooking soothes me. Allow me this comfort. Unless all this has completely spoiled your appetite?"

My stomach growled before I could speak, betraying any excuse I might make to let him, or myself, off the hook.

Vico grinned, the first truly easy expression I'd seen on his face in three days. "Your *stomaco* has spoken. We will sit outside, and you will pour more wine, yes?"

I sighed. "Only if you pick the bottle. Find a nice, expensive one. Francesca owes you at least that."

"Perfetto."

I let him dress the plates, then I grabbed cutlery and brought everything out to the patio while Vico hunted down one of Fran's good vintages. When he joined me outside it was with two fresh glasses and an unlabeled bottle of wine with a small piece of masking tape on it.

I eyed it sceptically. "That doesn't look expensive."

"It depends on how you define 'expensive.' This was made from Fiera Vista's own grapes. Francesca paid a local vintner handsomely to come up with a good blend, which she only brought out on special occasions. She only has a few bottles left. So, maybe not expensive, but rare. Will that do?"

"I bow to a superior sommelier."

Vico smiled and poured. "To setting aside old grudges."

"I can drink to that."

We clinked glasses, and dug into our pasta. Once again, Vico had created something light and summery that gave my tastebuds plenty to savor, and he'd made it look so easy. Maybe I should get more lessons from him.

Vico swallowed his pasta and looked at me, all serious all of a sudden. "*Allora*, will you be keeping Fiera Vista?"

I chewed on a piece of squid, trying to decide on how to answer. "I … haven't decided yet. I have to go over Fran's finances with Signore Galanti." I should be up front with him since he was so invested in my decision. "I can't afford to keep it on my salary alone. So it depends on whether Fran's savings are enough to keep it going."

Vico nodded. "I understand."

"I'll give you first right of refusal if I do wind up selling."

Vico chuckled. "And where do you think I am hiding two million euros?"

"Nonna might have a secret nest egg."

"Nonna is the least secretive person I know. But I appreciate your consideration."

By unspoken mutual agreement, we avoided the topic of the future of Fiera Vista for the rest of the evening. I plied Vico with wine, and he regaled me with stories from local lore, the feuds and vanities of the local landowners, each claiming to produce the best olives, the best wine, the best cheese—oh, no, the cheese from the next valley over is not edible, not at all, only cheese from here will do—who had stolen whose pig, who had warred with whom over the exact placement of their land's boundary line, so as to claim the tree where the best truffles grew.

He reassured me that Fran's last days had been good ones, her social life active and her health apparently decent right up to the evening she'd died in her sleep.

Vico's reserve from the last few days was gone, and I tried to puzzle out why. His reaction seemed odd. I'd have been either hopping mad or crushed if I'd thought I was about to become a millionaire and regain my family's heritage, and then had that wealth snatched from my hands.

The stars were dusting the sky when we both finally stood. Fireflies sparkled in the garden. I stretched, then grabbed the plates and brought them back to the kitchen.

"I'll deal with the dishes tomorrow," I said.

"*Va bene.*"

We both stood staring at each other awkwardly. "I guess this is good night, then."

"*Buona notte,* Elodia."

He leaned over, bussed my cheek in that polite way Europeans had of greeting or parting. But then he didn't quite lean away. I locked gazes with him, searching out an answer to a question neither of us had voiced aloud.

Then I leaned in myself and kissed him. He didn't pull away.

It started slowly, more tentative than our first time, neither of us sure of the other anymore. Yet there was no denying my body's reaction to him, nor his to mine. I clung to his shirt as he clasped my head, his hands threading through my hair, his lips hot against mine. I opened my mouth to let him in, and the floodgates threatened to burst apart, the desire I felt for him coursing through me, demanding release.

I wanted to know him, let my fingers explore every inch of his skin, every scar and mole and callus, have him map me in turn.

And yet …

I pressed my hands against his chest and stepped back.

"Maybe this isn't a good idea," I whispered.

"Is this not what you wanted, Elodia?"

"Yes. But …" I lifted my hands from his chest, my fingers stretching regretfully for one more touch. This wasn't the consequence-free romp I'd signed up for the other night. "There's … a lot going on right now. Maybe we should take it a little slower."

"Fine." But Vico's tone said it was anything but fine. He stepped back, scrubbed a hand through his hair, finally gave me a wry smile. "But this time, it is you who owe me dinner for leaving me in such a state."

"I—Deal. As long as you pick a restaurant, because you definitely don't want me to cook."

"OK. It's a date." Then he shook his head and disappeared into the night.

Despite the evening not being particularly muggy, I seriously considered jumping into the pool fully clothed to cool down. But as he'd kissed me, and I'd almost lost myself in his embrace, an ugly suspicion had wormed its way into my heart.

Vico had been hot, then cold, and then suddenly, against all common sense, hot again when I might have expected lukewarm at best, but more likely a deeper frostiness.

Sometimes, I hated the way my too analytical mind worked.

What if he didn't really want *me*, anymore? What if he just wanted my newly found money? Or worse, what if all that talk about setting aside old grudges was just that: talk?

What if he wanted revenge?

CHAPTER SEVEN

"This can't be right." I'd driven in to town to see Fran's banker, to introduce myself and prepare for putting the accounts in my name, but now …

The bank's investment adviser shrugged. "It is reality, signorina."

"But … there's supposed to be five million euros in these accounts."

"Signora Leduc transferred her investments elsewhere, I am afraid."

"Where?"

"That information was none of my affair, signorina. Once Signora Leduc took her business from us, we had no right to ask."

"But …"

"I sincerely wish to help you, signorina, but I cannot."

I sat back in my chair, staring in shocked silence at the investment statement before me. A grand total of 10,000 euros remained in Fran's accounts. Not even enough to cover the taxes on Fiera Vista.

"Thank you for your time, signore. I need to speak with my lawyer and I might still be in touch."

"I can assure you that all transactions made from this account were legitimate."

"I'm sure you can, but from my perspective, this money is now missing, and I need to figure out how to find it." I stood and took my leave.

Fran's money had vanished. Her artwork was nowhere to be found. Something smelled badly, badly wrong here.

CHAPTER EIGHT

AFTER returning from the bank, I called my boss, because it was clear I was going to need a few days more to review the estate with Signore Galanti, and ensure Fiera Vista was on sound enough fiscal footing.

"Ah, Élodie. I have some news. I was hoping to do this in person but sooner is better." Vikram didn't sound that hopeful. Uh-oh. "The contract for the latest prototype was suspended—one of the EU member governments pulled funding. The company tried to find appropriate roles for the affected employees, but unfortunately, some layoffs were unavoidable, and full-time employees take precedence over those in temporary positions. I'm afraid we were unable to find a new role for you."

"I—" My voice had a weird wobble to it. I'd never been laid off before. "I was just transferred to Varese. I guess there's no way to transfer back to Montréal?"

"Given the history there, HR did not feel it would be a good idea."

Fabulous. I was the one who agreed to leave town to escape an ugly situation with my old colleagues and now they got to keep their jobs. The job in Italy had been a straightforward horizontal move, with no apparent career ramifications, and what had initially looked like good upside potential.

Back home, I'd had an office romance with a peer—not explicitly disallowed by the corporate rules, as long as HR knew about it. But after my old boss repeatedly passed me over for promotion, I discovered that my lover had been taking personal credit for my design contributions—to the point of omitting me from the patent applications. I tried to set the record straight, but despite my extensive log book notes, it became clear my position had become untenable and my old boss wasn't going to take me seriously. "Throwing people under the bus isn't how we do things around here, Élodie, and Marc is a valuable member of the team."

With the writing on the wall, the opportunity to get out from a toxic situation without getting a reputation for being "difficult" had seemed like a rational choice, especially when weighed against the downside of creating a major scene. My industry wasn't that big and word traveled uncomfortably fast.

Now I wondered just how much my past had played into the choice to not find me an "appropriate" new role.

"Élodie? Of course there will be severance. But I will need you to sign some paperwork."

"What about my visa?" Was I going to get kicked out of

the country?

"It was valid for two years. We will need to notify Immigration of your change in job status, but I believe if you register as unemployed, they will often let you stay until the original expiry date."

I made a mental note to check on that. The last thing I needed right now was to get deported. "I'm not sure when I can make it back up to Varese. I was originally calling to extend my leave by a few days. I didn't expect to have to deal with my aunt's estate."

"I'll email you the documents. You can come in to retrieve your personal items at your convenience. And Élodie—I'm sorry. Your work has been exemplary. Please feel free to use me as a reference."

"Thanks Vikram." What else was there to say?

"Goodbye, Élodie."

"Bye."

Oh man. My hands were shaking and my knees felt a little wobbly, so I headed to the kitchen to fortify myself with a fresh cup of coffee. I had done nothing wrong, and yet a sense of shame washed over me. I'd lost my job. I wasn't good enough to keep around.

Stop it, El. It's not your fault the entire budget disappeared.

I told myself not to panic. There'd be severance.

But the sheer mountain of bureaucratic I-dotting and T-crossing facing me suddenly crashed down around me in a pile of forms, signatures, and to-do lists. The layoff package. Benefits. My visa. The Varese apartment. Résumé refreshing.

Job hunting. Signore Galanti. The Diva. The problems with the estate.

Breathe, El. Just breathe.

There was too much to think about. Too much going haywire in too few days. In a fit of restless energy, I located my swimsuit, changed, and then dove into Fran's—I still couldn't think of it as my—pool. The cool water snapped me out of my shock. For the first few laps, I set myself a furious pace, burning off my anger at the company in pure physical exertion. As I calmed down, I returned to my usual easy crawl, the rhythm of my strokes and breathing grounding me and letting me think.

Did I need to make any immediate decisions? Now that I had Fiera Vista, maybe I could break the lease on my Varese apartment and live here. According to Signore Galanti, that would also help with the estate tax situation, as I'd owe significantly less if I made Fiera Vista my primary residence instead of simply selling it. There was nothing to hurry back to in Varese now, so I could take a proper amount of time to figure out what I wanted to do with the estate, and where all the money had gone. I hadn't even been in the country long enough to unpack all my boxes from the initial trans-Atlantic move.

But with Fran's investments gone AWOL, I might not have enough funds to keep the estate going for very long. I should find out how long I needed to own Fiera Vista before I could sell it to avoid the transfer tax. A beautiful Tuscan villa was nice and all, unless it bankrupted me.

I kicked my legs harder. The swim was supposed to relax me, not stress me out even more.

A shadow fell across the pool and when I reached the end of my lap, Vico stood at the edge, watching me swim. I stopped, treading water in the deep end. "What's up?"

"I came to discuss some matters pertaining to the farm. But I see you are busy."

"I was hoping to do a few more lengths, but maybe we can still talk while I swim?" I kicked off from the far end and resumed my laps, this time with a casual breast stroke that kept my head above water.

"*Va bene.*" Vico kicked off his shoes and sat down at the end of the pool, dangling his legs in the water. "Francesca always had fresh produce delivered from the market. I assume you will want to discontinue these shipments since you are returning to Varese?"

So much for not making any immediate decisions. "Is it a lot of food?"

"No. A woman of Francesca's age doesn't eat much."

"Then don't cancel yet. I … may be here for a while." My face twisted in a grimace.

Vico stared at me as I made another round of the pool. "You look upset."

Was there any reason not to tell him? "That's because losing one's job is upsetting."

"I am sorry, Elodia. This is recent news?"

"Not even an hour old."

"Is there anything I can do?"

"This is my problem, Vico."

"OK!" He threw his hands up in a placating gesture and I realized my tone might not have been the friendliest. I stopped my laps and swam towards where he sat at the shallow end of the pool.

"I'm sorry, Vico. I didn't mean to snap at you. I'm just a little freaked out." And angry. The laps had taken the edge off but there was still a slow burn permeating my mood.

"Did you have any warning?"

"None. Unexpected budget cuts."

"*Ai*. Can you still afford dinner?"

"I'm unemployed, Vico, not broke." Yet.

"Good. Because while you may have been done an injustice, the only one of concern to me is how you left me last night." He stared at the cleavage of my swimsuit, and my nipples hardened at the look in his eyes.

I moved closer, closed my hand on his calf. "You're still bothered by that?"

He glanced down at his crotch. "I am more than bothered."

I was feeling frayed, and reckless, my misgivings of the night before subsumed by a need to belong to someone—anyone, anywhere—after being so abruptly cut loose. "That can be remedied."

I slid my hand up out of the water, along the side of his leg and over his knees, trailing drops of cool liquid along his skin. Vico tensed.

"Tell me to stop and I will."

Vico remained silent.

I slipped my fingers beneath his shorts, the coarse hairs along his thighs tickling my palm. Thrust my arm further until I pressed my hand against the bulge in his underwear. He sucked in a breath. I worked my fingers across the cotton fabric, massaging slowly as he hardened beneath me, my gaze never leaving his.

"What happened to taking things slowly, Elodia?"

"I guess everything speeds up when I don't know if they'll kick me out of the country tomorrow. What happened to worrying about what Nonna will think?"

"She grows more and more bitter. I do not want that for myself. Nonna's war with Francesca is in the past. You and I, Elodia—we are the opposite of enemies. At least, we could be." He covered my hand with his over his shorts, pausing my ministrations. "But you are angry. I would not have you regret this later."

"Will you?" I peered into his face, suddenly sure of my answer. "My job. The will. Nonna—they all feel like excuses to deny ourselves what I think we both want. Unless I'm mistaken?" I spread my fingers against his crotch. "Do you want me, Vico?"

In answer, he pushed my hand harder against his cock, and I resumed my massage. He spread his legs, and I snugged in between them, right up to the edge of the pool. He was fully hard beneath my fingers now. With my free hand, I undid the button at his waist, and zipped down his fly. Then I reached in as I slid my other hand out of his shorts, and freed his cock from his boxers.

"Elodia, what are you doing to me?"

"I think that's obvious, no?"

He shivered as I grasped his shaft, my hand still cool from the water. He leaned back, his breathing coming a little faster now as I rubbed up and down his length.

"I'm assuming you don't have a condom on you." I leaned closer. "Are you healthy?"

"*Sì.*"

"Well OK then." And I circled my tongue around the tip of his penis, before taking it in my mouth.

Vico threw his head back and groaned. I held the base of his shaft in one hand and continued to massage him while I sucked and licked. I slid the other hand back into the waistband of his boxers, caressing his ass as I bent over him. I closed my eyes, enjoying his small noises of pleasure. Vico's hips came up to greet me as I built a rhythm, swirling my tongue around his girth. He threaded his fingers through my hair, urging me on. I tasted salt as he came closer to release.

"El—Elodia! Ah!" Vico pushed my head away, and his hips jerked as he ejaculated into the pool.

I rested my arm on his thigh as he caught his breath. He reached down and tilted my chin up, running his thumb across my lips. "We are well matched, *tesoro.*" His hand moved down my throat, plunging beneath my swimsuit. He brushed his fingers against my nipple and I inhaled. He tensed, I thought to push off and jump into the pool with me, when we both heard it.

"Vico? Dove sei?" Nonna's voice echoed from the front of the house.

Vico surged up, quickly tucking himself away and fastening his shorts. He might say he didn't care about what Nonna thought, but—since she already believed I was a foreign hussy—I guess that didn't extend to being caught in a blow job. Probably wise. There were more tactful ways to break the news to Nonna. Ones less likely to result in Italian four-letter words.

I splashed water at him.

"What are you doing?" He glared at me.

"Your shorts look a little suspicious right now." I nodded at the spots my arms had dripped on.

Vico grunted. "Ah. Maybe do it again then."

I kicked away from the pool wall, spraying him generously. "You can say you surprised me, and I overreacted."

Vico arched an eyebrow. "That would not entirely be a lie." He turned towards the house. *"Sono qui fuori, Nonna!"*

Nonna trundled into view, frowning as she caught sight of me. She waved at him to come join her.

Vico shot me a glance. "We still have our discussion to finish. I should take you on a tour of the farm."

"I'll go dry off and get changed."

"Va bene. I will only be a few minutes."

But when I returned downstairs from my room, clothed and ready for anything, an empty house greeted me. A small piece of paper lay on the kitchen counter.

Nonna needed a ride into town. We will talk later. —Vico
Right. I guess that left me with my to-do list, then.

CHAPTER NINE

The next day, I dealt with my termination papers, then made a few calls, trying to figure out the best way to handle my lease and a potential move. I'd rented a furnished apartment on a month-to-month lease, with a plan to find something a little more permanent once I'd settled in and learned a bit more about the Varese area. I guess that had been a wiser plan than I'd realized at the time. It was the start of the month, so if I moved now I'd lose almost a full month's rent, but I could live with that.

The busywork kept my mind off Vico, and what might have happened had Nonna not interrupted us. Those were sexy daydreams, but now that I'd gotten over the initial shock and anger at the layoff, I wondered if Nonna hadn't come in just at the right time to save me from myself.

I couldn't deny that I wanted Vico badly. Vico was the estate's manager, and I'd been thinking of the property still as Fran's. But it belatedly occurred to me that I was now his employer. I'd avoided office entanglements in Varese for a reason—my last one having stalled my career. And now I was the one in the position of more power. So my attraction predated my understanding of our actual ties. So he seemed equally attracted to me. Was that any kind of excuse?

The whole situation with the will and Nonna made things doubly fraught.

It also didn't help that when I looked at people who were well placed to have disappeared Fran's money and art, Vico stood near the top of the list. I didn't want to think that of him, and I'd seen nothing at the cottage or in the manner in which he and Nonna lived to suggest that they'd come into money themselves. But I couldn't help my suspicions, and I couldn't let myself be naïve just because of my attraction to him. I just couldn't figure out how to broach the topic with Vico delicately. I'd likely sound the death knell on any expansion of our relationship the minute I tried.

I'd run out of busywork. Time to go find the Diva and see if I could figure out why she wouldn't start, especially if I needed to head back to Varese to tie up loose ends.

Vico had rolled my motorcycle out of his truck and into a barn halfway down the driveway, saying he would bring up some tools from his own workshop, so I went to see if he'd made good on that promise. Walking down the driveway, the Tuscan summer sun warmed my face as bees and butterflies wove their way through the wheat fields to either side. At the barn, I lifted the latch on the door, fumbling for the light switch in the sudden shift from outdoor bright to indoor dim. I gasped as I took in the sight before me. *What the actual—*

The Diva had been eviscerated, scattered pieces of engine lying on the floor and a workbench. I clapped a hand to my mouth. She was still under warranty!

Not anymore, El.

My shoulders hunched as the mess sank in. It would take days to put her back together. What had Vico been thinking? A near-new Ducati, my one splurge since moving. Disemboweled in a dilapidated old barn.

I howled in frustration, then released a despairing cackle, which quickly turned to sobs. My gutted motorcycle was the perfect symbol for the shattered pieces of my life. No family. No job. A relationship—if I could even call it that—probably going nowhere and an inheritance that might or might not ruin me financially.

"Elodia? What is the matter?"

I hadn't heard Vico come in. I stared up at him from where I'd sagged to the floor. "What's the matter? What's the *matter?* You destroyed my bike, Vico! Who the hell gave you permission to take it apart like that? Do you know how much that thing cost? Do you have any idea how to put it back together?" I heard myself, heard the irrational, whiny note in my voice, and it just made me feel worse.

He crouched down next to me, reached out to put a comforting hand on my shoulder, but I swatted it away. "Calm down, Elodia, I can expl—"

"Don't you fucking tell me to 'calm down.' I'm allowed to be angry, goddammit." If there was one thing I was not going to put up with, it was another man telling me I was overreacting. *The company can't help you if you make a fuss, Élodie. Think of the optics, Élodie. It's not worth ruining careers over, Élodie. Just sign the nondisclosure, Élodie.*

Vico cocked his head. "You are right, Elodia. I am too used to just fixing the farm vehicles myself. I should have asked you first."

His simple acknowledgement took all the piss out of my vinegar. The motorcycle wasn't the problem. Vico wasn't the problem. This, here, was just the catalyst for a chain reaction of anger at all the other stressors in my life right now. Vico didn't deserve this from me. I'd lashed out for the wrong reasons, at the wrong person.

I swiped the moisture from my cheeks brusquely. "No, *I'm* sorry, Vico. You were just trying to help. I reacted badly. Did you at least figure out what was wrong?"

"I think so. Did you perhaps drop your key on the road that day?"

I thought back to the ride. I'd stopped to take a picture by the side of the road. "I did, actually."

"I think you broke the antenna in your key. The chip in the key itself is fine, but it cannot talk to the control panel when you insert it in the ignition. But when you hold the key next to the control panel, everything lights up."

Fancy computer-assisted ignitions. What a bizarre failure mode. "So I just need a new key?"

"Not even that, although now the bike is more complicated to start."

"And you had to take the whole bike apart to figure that

out?"

"I thought it was a simple mechanical problem. But I eliminated all those."

"How *did* you find it?"

"By chance. On Youtube."

I blew out a big breath, trying to get a grip on myself. That *did* sound esoteric. Vico stood up and held out a hand to help me up. I clasped it and let him tug me upright, finding myself chest to chest with him as dust motes swirled around us in the musty barn. He brushed a stray strand of hair from my cheek, his fingers feathering against my skin. "Am I forgiven, *straniera?*"

I snorted softly. "Only if the Diva starts after you put her back together."

Vico smiled. "That is fair."

"There's something else." I couldn't put it off any longer.

"What is it, Elodia? I do not like this look on your face."

There was no good way to go about this, so I just plunged right in. "Do you know where Fran's artwork went?"

"The paintings?" Vico frowned, stared into space as though visualizing them in his head. "I had not noticed. But now that you say this thing …" His puzzled expression looked so sincere. I so wanted to trust it. "They are not in the house, are they?"

"No. They're just gone." I bit my lip.

"There is something else, something you do not want to tell me."

"I …"

"Just say it, Elodia."

"Her money's gone too. There's … there's almost nothing left to cover Fiera Vista's monthly outlays."

"*Ai.* We will get something for next week's harvest, but I will have to pay the workers."

"Did you have any signing control on her accounts?"

Vico's mouth tightened. "What are you asking, Élodie? You think I could do this thing? Steal from Francesca?"

I looked anywhere but at him. "I don't know what to think, Vico. After everything you told me about our families, I can understand if you wanted payback. But …"

He put his fingers to my chin, turning and tilting my head until I had to return his gaze. "But?"

I'd expected an explosion. An angry denial. Not this hurt disappointment. And suddenly I knew in my bones that my trust in him wasn't misplaced. Vico was the real thing: an honest man. Someone you counted on in a crisis. The kind of person who spent hours taking your whole bike apart just to save you a few hundred bucks. Who, despite being an accomplished chef, made sure his grandmother got recipe credit. "But I don't believe you capable of hurting Fran." I swallowed. "Or me."

He stared at me, seeking out the truth of my words in my eyes.

I shrugged. "Besides, I think Nonna would kill you if she caught you stealing."

He let out a sharp chuckle, and wrapped me in a quick, tight hug. "There, you are very right, *straniera.*" Then he bent down to kiss me.

I put my fingers to his lips. "Vico. What happened before
—"

He nibbled on my fingertips, and my insides turned to
mush. "*Sì*. I have a new fondness for that pool."

"I need to apologize, Vico."

He leaned back a bit. *"Perché?"*

"I—if I own Fiera Vista now, that means I'm your boss.
It shouldn't have happened. It was wrong of me."

"Is that the problem? You believe you have sexually
harassed me?"

"Vico—"

"No, *straniera*. What you say is *ridicolo*. It would only be
wrong if the attention is not welcome. And you have seen the
proof that I welcome your attentions." He pressed his hips to
mine. "You can even feel it now, if you like."

"Vico, I think—"

"*Ai*. Before, you say we think too much. Now, you want
to think more. The time for thinking is past, no?"

My hands were pressed against his chest, fingers splayed
against the cotton of his shirt. I wanted to succumb to his
words. But I didn't trust my emotional state right now. "Let's
—" Outside, tires crunched on the gravel driveway. We both
turned our heads to follow their progress. "Let's go see who
that is, and then maybe you can take me on that tour of the
farm."

"Fine. But think on this: you think too much." Before I
could turn to go, he clasped my nape and pulled me to him,

kissing me deeply, his lips like velvet against mine. He broke away, heading for the door. "Here in Italia, *l'amore* comes from the heart, not the head. Or is it not the same in Canada?"

As we trekked back up to the villa, I contemplated his words. I'd jumped right in with both feet when I thought Vico was just a lark, a brief fling without strings before returning to Varese. But Vico wasn't a plaything, however good he made me feel. Our families were intertwined, knotted together by old entanglements and betrayals. I couldn't just ignore all that history.

He might have gotten over his own reluctance, but I kept seesawing between enthusiasm and hesitation, my physical attraction to him held in check by justified caution. A caution I'd only abandoned because I was still reeling from loss.

A caution impossible to heed the moment I felt the heat of his skin beneath my lips and fingertips.

Someone save me from Etruscan gods brought to life.

Someone save me from myself.

Three minutes and we reached the top of the drive, where a nondescript beige sedan and a sleek black Mercedes had parked near the front entrance. Signore Mirri, Fran's sleazy "friend" from the funeral reception, stood at the entrance with a man I didn't recognize. The stranger held a sheaf of papers in his hand, and Mirri tapped his foot impatiently at our approach.

"Ah! Signorina Martel. Good, good. You will hand over the keys, please."

"I beg your pardon?"

"This is my lawyer, Signore Bertolo. He assures me the paperwork is all in order."

"Paperwork for what?"

"Why, the property transfer, of course. Did Signore Galanti not tell you? The estate is mine."

"I believe there's been some kind of misunderstanding. My aunt left everything to me."

"I am afraid you have been misled. That testament is out of date. I am in possession of a document testifying to my dearest Francesca's last wishes. She wanted me to enjoy my final years in this place where we lived our finest moments. We were so close, you see."

I glanced at Vico, and the naked disbelief on his face told me everything I needed to know. "Let me see those papers." I practically snatched them from Bertolo's hands.

I scanned them quickly. All the legalese was in Italian, so I handed these to Vico to translate for me. One handwritten letter in English stood out: in a shaky, fine script, the writer did indeed wish to "leave all my worldly goods, including Fiera Vista, to my beloved Gianni Mirri. —Francesca Leduc"

I cast my mind back to the birthday cards Fran had occasionally sent. It *could* be her handwriting, but something felt off.

Mirri smirked. "You see? Be a good girl and give me the keys."

I squared my shoulders. "I'm afraid I can't do that. I'll have to speak to Signore Galanti first. He's already begun the transfer process to me, and he will have to review this paperwork before I let you set one foot inside that house."

Mirri gave me an oily smile. "I was afraid you would dispute this. Bertolo?"

The lawyer handed me yet another paper, also in Italian. I stepped away from Mirri and Bertolo, dragging Vico with me. "What does this say?"

Vico scanned it quickly. "It is an order for you to immediately vacate the premises while this dispute is settled in court."

"Can they do that?"

"It has been signed by the proper authority so I believe so, yes."

I turned back to Mirri. "Is this really necessary?"

"You are a foreigner with few ties to this country. I cannot risk any valuable items in the house going missing when they are mine by right."

I bristled at his implication. "Do you mean the valuable items you've already removed from the premises?" Because the certainty now filled me that Mirri had already ransacked the estate. I'd never doubt Vico again. "If I'm not allowed in there while this is under review then you aren't either." People like him who worried about what other people might do generally did so because it was something they could see themselves doing. Over my dead body would I give him the keys to this place.

"I am afraid you have no say in the matter, signorina."

"We'll see about that. I am going inside to call Signore

Galanti. You two can wait out here."

"You will be going inside to pack, signorina."

"That too. I suppose you'll want to inspect my bags." Although what they thought I could squirrel away in two motorcycle bags was beyond me. I stomped into the house.

Vico followed me into the foyer and shut the door in Mirri's face. He waved one of the papers at me. "Elodia, there is something else."

"What's that?"

"It is an eviction notice. For me and Nonna."

"I thought they can't do that because of the covenant."

"It seems they are going to try anyway."

"Fuck that noise."

I stalked up the stairs to my room, to find my phone and call Galanti, all the while trying to figure out how to expose Gianni Mirri for the thieving gold-digger I now had no doubt he was.

CHAPTER TEN

I tossed my bags onto the bed in the cottage's guest room, which was about a third of the size of my room at the villa. Nonna's plaintive voice drifted up from downstairs, as Vico's soft tenor explained the situation to her. She occasionally punctuated her questions with outraged exclamations. *'No! Impossibile!'*

If she didn't like the idea of me owning Fiera Vista, she liked the idea of being beholden to Mirri even less.

Signore Galanti agreed that under no circumstances was I to give Mirri the keys to Fiera Vista. We both believed he'd waste no time in setting up shop squatting amid Fran's possessions—a plan I couldn't really blame Mirri for because it had been mine first. Galanti would go to court first thing in the morning, which would hopefully let me back into the house I'd agreed to vacate under the condition that Mirri postpone Vico and Nonna's eviction. That little piece of horsetrading had kept Bertolo from calling in the local authorities to boot me out forcibly.

One part of me wanted to just walk away—leave Fiera Vista to Mirri, let him deal with the taxes, the upkeep, everything. It would simplify my life enormously. I could return to Montréal, continue my job hunt, resume the career that had gotten sidetracked, and wash my hands of all these complications.

But another part of me yearned to stay. The part that longed to get closer to Vico. The part that didn't want to see Nonna turned out of the only home she'd ever known. The part that couldn't stand the idea of a slimeball like Mirri getting his hands on anything of Fran's. The part that had fallen in love with Italy in only a few short weeks.

I just couldn't figure out how to pay for a protracted legal fight I stood a decent chance at losing.

I made my way downstairs, hoping to express my gratitude to Nonna for allowing me to stay here until I could find a place in town. It was high tourist season and my initial calls to the local hotels had proven fruitless. It was too early in my decision-making process to consider a longer-term local rental.

I found Nonna and Vico still deep in discussion.

"Bah!" Nonna threw up her hands and hurried off to the kitchen as soon as she saw me.

Vico sighed. "She's very upset."

"She knows I'm not the enemy, right?"

"*Non siamo neppure amiche,*" Nonna shouted from the kitchen.

"*Il nemico del nemico è mio amico,*" Vico shot back. The

enemy of my enemy is my friend.

"*Che palle!*"

I'd looked that one up on Google Translate after that first day. Nonna had a bit of a mouth on her.

"Listen, it's still light out. We're not allowed in the house but nobody said the grounds were off limits. Still want to give me that tour of the farm?" I needed to arm myself with a little more knowledge before I talked to Signore Galanti next, and sound out Vico about a few things without Nonna swearing and muttering every time she caught sight of me.

Vico nodded, and we headed out. He pointed out Nonna's extensive vegetable garden, and talked about the wheat fields blanketing the hillside. The golden sheafs of wheat swayed in the breeze. "We will harvest next week, then work the fields and leave them until replanting in the fall." Vico grimaced. "Or not, depending on Signore Mirri."

And my cash flow.

We walked past the building housing the Diva. "This is one of our storage barns." He pointed up the hill at another cluster of buildings. "Those are the others. For equipment and the like."

"Vico, did you see Fran a lot?"

"Yes. Almost daily. She liked me to cook for her."

"Was Mirri with her often?"

"I would have called him more of an acquaintance than a dear friend. He came and went."

With Fran's paintings, apparently. "So, they weren't lovers like he's implied?"

"I cannot say for sure. She did not spend all her time here at Fiera Vista. She would visit friends in Firenze, sometimes for weeks at a time." He glanced at me. "And as to what she did in the evenings after I was gone, I cannot say. But he rarely stayed the night."

"Right. So he's most likely pulling some kind of con, here."

"I would guess the same. Do you plan to fight him?"

"I—want to? I'm just not sure I have the resources."

We walked past the villa, both of us lost in our own thoughts, until we arrived at the olive grove. The silver-green leaves on the trees rustled in the wind, their gnarled bark making them look ancient and wise, although they probably weren't that old.

"It's beautiful up here." The fruit on the trees was still small.

"That tree there?" Vico pointed to a tree with a significantly larger trunk than most. "It is over 500 years old. Maybe 1000."

I walked up to it, pressed my hand against its trunk, tried to absorb some of its serenity, bottle it up inside me to see me through the whirlwind.

Vico came up behind me, swept the hair from my nape, and played his lips along my neck. I shivered, instantly aroused. "Vico …"

He wrapped his arms around my waist, pulling me close. His voice rumbled low in my ear. "I do not know whether to hate Signore Mirri or thank him. If he wins, I have no home.

But also if he wins, you will not be my *padrona*, and we can stop pretending we do not want each other."

I twisted in his arms until I was facing him, staring up into those icicle eyes of his, impossibly warm for such a wintry color. "With the ownership of Fiera Vista contested like this, one could argue I'm not your boss right now."

"I like the way you think, *straniera*."

"I like the way you feel."

We both leaned in at the same time, logic and emotion merging in the soft clash of our lips. As we kissed, I wondered how many other lovers that olive tree had witnessed twining beneath its branches, and if all of them had been as drunk with desire as me.

CHAPTER ELEVEN

I broke the kiss for air, and we touched foreheads, breathing hard.

Vico took my hand. "Come with me."

He led me back through the grove, and we stopped only to steal another deep kiss at the gate. We approached Fiera Vista.

"Vico, we're not allowed in the house."

"They did not forbid us the pool house." He pulled me along the patio, took a ring of keys from his pocket and unlocked the cabana. He cracked the door open, then paused. "Wait here. Or go inside if you wish. I will return shortly."

He made his way to the villa, unlocked one of the patio doors, and slipped inside. I bit my lip, irrationally afraid that Mirri would jump out of the bushes and catch Vico where he'd agreed not to be. When Vico finally reappeared, I breathed a sigh of relief. He was carrying a tall, narrow green bottle.

"I think I'm high enough on you that I don't need wine."

I stroked my hand up his bicep as he reached me.

Vico leaned in and kissed the hollow behind my jaw, pulling me inside the cabana. "It is not wine." He leaned away and held up the bottle. "It is oil from Il Vecchio, the old tree in the orchard. Mirri will not know to miss it."

I stared at the bottle. "Don't say that name again tonight."

"Not to worry, *straniera*. Very soon, neither of us will be saying much." His eyes blazed cold fire beneath his feathery bangs.

I reached up, scrubbed my fingers against the stubble of his cheek, up past his ear and through his silky hair. I pulled his mouth down to mine and all thoughts of Mirri fled.

Vico set the bottle down on the coffee table. He wrapped his arms around me, enveloping me in his heat, running his hands across my back and shoulders. He found the edge of my shirt, tugged it up and over my head, and tossed it to the floor, so I returned the favor, eager to feel his skin beneath my palms.

He had a farmer's tan, the skin of his arms darker than his chest. I put both hands on his flanks and drew them slowly upward, admiring the sweep of his well-defined pecs, muscles he'd obtained from honest hard work, not a gym. His nipples tugged against the webbing between my fingers as I brushed my hands across them.

Vico exhaled softly at my touch, his eyes half-lidded. He released the clasp of my bra, skimmed his fingers up and over my shoulders, teasing the straps down until the fabric fell away between us.

We stood like that, each taking in the other's body, stroking the other's skin, mirroring the other's soft touches, trailing exploratory fingers over warm flesh. He cupped my breasts, grazing his thumbs over my nipples, setting my nerve endings alight, and I did the same for him, watching his eyes go hazy with each new touch.

He kissed my forehead, played his lips along my brow, then leaned away and picked up the oil bottle. "It is time for a tasting."

"Now?" I tilted my head. I was jonesing for a taste, but not of olive oil. "Straight?"

"Fine Tuscan olive oil is like wine—each with its own bouquet, consistency, and flavor." Vico smiled slyly. "But we will not be sampling it the traditional way."

He twisted off the cap, poured oil into his palm, and then slathered it over his chest. His skin gleamed in the soft light, slick with the liquid as I watched the play of his massaging fingers.

"Don't you want a taste, Elodia?"

I made a small noise of assent and bent my head, taking his nipple in my mouth. The slightly bitter taste of the oil burst across my tongue with a richness of flavor that melded with and complimented the scent of his skin. His hand came to the side of my throat, pressing me close while I licked and sucked on this unexpected feast, his body straining towards my lips in response.

Then, as I continued to lap at his chest, he poured more oil into his hands and coated my breasts, spreading the oil in slow circles. He swept his hands up towards my throat and along my shoulders, then back down, his fingers gliding like silk across my lubricated pores. As he turned his attentions to my nipples, squeezing lightly, I gave a muffled moan, and slid my own hands down his torso, searching out another source for mutual pleasure.

I popped the button on his jeans and reached in, pressing my hand against his cock. As I stroked it, Vico's hands skimmed from my breasts up beneath my jaw, tilting my head up so he could get his own taste. I let my head hang back as he kissed my throat, lost in his lips and tongue and the heat of him hardening against my fingers.

We pressed against each other, our torsos slippery with oil, warm and slick and satiny soft. His skin sliding against mine made me wild to feel more of him. It was time. I pushed his jeans and briefs down, and by mutual agreement, we were both quickly naked.

Vico held up the oil bottle. "More?"

I bit my lip and nodded.

"Lie down."

The pool house, doubling as a guest house, was fully furnished, with a bed behind a screen separating the sleeping space from a small sitting space. But my lust-addled brain still spared a thought for cleaning up all this oil. I grabbed a couple of thick towels from the stack by the door and draped them, then myself, over a long chaise instead of the bed.

Vico knelt over me, drizzled oil over my stomach and thighs, and, as I held out my hands, into my waiting palms.

And then we did nothing but revel in each other's touch for long minutes at a time.

I reached up and poured the contents of my hands onto his back, working the oil into his shoulders as he massaged my belly and kneaded my thighs, trailing my hands down to coat his ass, my hands working in long strokes. The oil smoothed out the scratchiness of the calluses on Vico's palms, and I spread my legs for him as his hands moved up and down my thighs in a slow rhythm that made me strain towards him.

"Vico …"

"*Si, straniera?*"

"Make love to me."

Vico smiled. "I thought that was what I was doing. You North Americans are so impatient." But he produced a condom and sheathed himself. Then he bent down, his hair brushing my mound, and kissed my cunt long and deep.

"Vico …" But the word was barely a hoarse whisper. I gripped the towel as his tongue played havoc with my nerve endings, swirling around my clit and teasing the nub. Then he sucked and pulled at it, his insistent mouth driving me to wild distraction.

I came in a quick paroxysm, and I was still shaking and crying out when Vico pulled himself on top of me, his tongue gliding from cunt to breast in one long stroke. He took my breast in his mouth, sucking at the nipple in the exact rhythm he'd used below, and in the same beat entered me.

I grabbed his head, brought his mouth to mine, devoured it hungrily. Then as he began to move within me, I wrapped my arms and legs around him, the oil making him almost impossible to grasp. I squirmed against him, the almost frictionless sensation of his skin against mine decadent and inebriating. My tongue flicked against his shoulders, his throat, his chest, addicted to the flavor of the oil and the small gasps each lick induced from him.

We flowed against each other, my hips undulating, his pumping, hands sliding across skin, lips and mouths and tongues tasting greedily.

And then he came, gasping out my name, and I muffled his cries with my kisses as he exploded within me.

Vico withdrew from me, swept my sticky hair from my cheeks, nuzzled the side of my neck, resting on an elbow as he dipped a hand between my legs. I turned my head to kiss him, tonguing him relentlessly as his rubbing fingers brought me to new heights, and I orgasmed in a long sigh.

I clasped his head between my still-oily hands. "You were right. We are well matched."

Vico buried his nose in my palm, then fixed me with those crystal clear eyes of his. "How do you say in English? Maybe 'the jury is still out?' "

"How so?" I couldn't hide a slightly worried pout.

"What is your opinion of showering together?"

I grinned. "When there's this much oil to rinse off, I'm definitely in favor."

The skin around Vico's eyes crinkled. "Then we are well

matched *di sicuro*." He pushed himself up and held out a hand to me. "Come. The water is hot."

"And so are you." I clapped my hand over my mouth as Vico arched an eyebrow at me. "I said that out loud, didn't I?"

"So what? You are hot too, *tesoro*."

"As long as we're both getting inflated heads."

Vico pressed a kiss against my temple and tugged me towards the bathroom. "I believe we are both getting exactly what we want."

I couldn't argue with that.

CHAPTER TWELVE

As we walked back down the drive to the cottage, hands entwined, I basked in the warm afterglow of great sex and even better company. The cypresses towered above us, tall sentries marking our path.

"Vico …"

"Yes, *straniera?*"

"If Fiera Vista was yours, what would you do with it?"

"Are you asking me if I would sell?"

"Is that what you'd do?"

Our feet crunched on the gravel for a few steps before he answered. "No. I would keep it."

"You'd move you and Nonna up to the villa and live there?"

"I would convert it to *agriturismo*—there would not need to be many changes. The villa has enough rooms for guests, and the pool house is perfect for those who want more privacy. I would renovate one of the barns for olive oil and wine tasting. Maybe even start a small restaurant."

"Wow. That sounds perfect for you."

"Maybe. Except I do not have a head for numbers. And the banks here, it is very hard to get loans from them, for—how do you say?—seed capital. I do not have enough of my own money for this."

"I see." We were almost back at the cottage.

"I made a business plan for Francesca once, but she told me my numbers were no good."

"Right." I squeezed his hand. "Do you still have that plan lying around? Can I see it?"

"But the numbers—"

"I'm an engineer, Vico. I manage multimillion-euro projects. If there's anything I've got, it's a head for numbers." I turned to face him. "I'm going to need your help if I'm going to fight Mirri. Maybe we can help each other. What do you say?"

"I still like the way you think, *straniera*."

And with that, we were facing the cottage door, and I braced myself for an evening of side-eye from Nonna.

It was easier going in with an ally.

CHAPTER THIRTEEN

WHEN I got up the next morning, I found a sheaf of papers leaning against the guest room door: Vico's business plan for Fiera Vista. I flipped through it quickly but a cursory examination didn't tell me what might have caused Fran to nix the project's financial viability. A part of me suspected her advancing years were the real reason and she just hadn't wanted to tell Vico she simply didn't feel like starting a new venture at her age. I'd look the plans over later when I had more time, but right now, I needed to find my way to Signore Galanti's office as quickly as possible.

Vico had gotten up early to coordinate the haying, and Nonna was pottering away in her garden. I grabbed some muesli for breakfast, snatched up a set of keys and borrowed the small hatchback Vico had as an alternative to the farm truck—Fran's Mercedes now being off limits—and drove into Poggibonsi.

An unpleasant surprise lurked in wait for me outside Galanti's office: Signore Mirri.

"Ah, Signorina Martel. I was hoping to catch you before you went in."

"I'm not speaking to you without my lawyer present. Where's Bertolo, by the way?" Mirri's attorney was nowhere in sight.

"He will be joining us shortly, but I thought it would be more productive for you and I to speak directly."

"I told you: not without my lawyer."

"Signorina, please. I am trying to save you money and time. I know you do not have the means to pay for the maintenance of such a fine estate as Fiera Vista. I can mire you in court filings for years. Unless …" He paused, deliberately stretching out the reveal of what he considered my salvation.

I tapped my foot, left him hanging.

"… Unless you can see fit to selling me Fiera Vista. I will make you a very fair price."

And there it was. He probably didn't have a case, the bastard. I suddenly had no doubt that every single document he'd supplied to support his claim was forged or of other questionable provenance. And that his "fair price" would be well below market value.

But he wasn't wrong. He could make my life miserable, tying me up in knots before the gears of the Italian judicial system ground into motion.

"Get out of my way, Mirri."

"Signorina …"

I brushed past him into Galanti's office. "You can lay

your case out in front of my lawyer, or not at all."

Mirri oozed into the waiting room behind me while I found the most isolated seat possible so I didn't have to sit near him. I buried my face in my phone, ignoring Bertolo when he arrived five minutes later. Another five interminable minutes tortoised by before Galanti ushered us into his office. The niceties of greetings dispensed with, Galanti and Bertolo started jabbering away in staccato Italian, with Mirri interjecting here and there.

"Stop." I interrupted firmly before the conversation got too involved. "We're doing this in English or not at all."

Mirri smirked. "The courts will not speak to you in English, signorina."

"We're not in court. And this conversation is over unless I can understand it."

Galanti nodded. "Of course, signorina. My apologies. I was just trying to be expedient but I can see that was wrong."

Damn straight. I was his *client, for fuck's sake.*

Bertolo laid out for us their legal plan, minus Mirri's extortionate demand. They did indeed intend to keep me busy in court for the foreseeable future. When they were done, Galanti saw them out, since I refused to shake their hands. He sat back down across from me.

"How good is their case?"

"I cannot say before I have an expert look over this supposed testament from Signora Leduc."

I told Galanti about Mirri's offer—sell and he'd drop the case. "He must know he can't win. He's just trying to squeeze me."

"That is as may be, signorina. But you will still have to decide how to proceed. A protracted fight in the courts will cost money, which you will not be able to take from the estate."

"There is no money in the estate." I brought Galanti up to speed on Fran's bank accounts.

"But this is not right! Signora Leduc was a rich woman."

"And elderly, rich women attract leeches like Mirri."

"You believe he is a thief as well as a fraud?"

"I'm pretty sure there's only one way to find out."

"Yes, signorina. I will look into this immediately. And I am ever so sorry this is happening to you. I have never seen its like in all my years."

"Yes, well. It's not your fault. The only thing to do now is hire a good forensic accountant."

Unless I could kneecap Mirri's case somehow.

And then there was the small matter of what to do should the estate truly become mine.

Selling would certainly get rid of a whole heap of hassle.

And lose me Vico in the bargain. Something I was starting to think might be the bigger disaster.

CHAPTER FOURTEEN

I lay on my stomach on my bed in the cottage's guest bedroom, studying my laptop screen. I'd asked Vico for a soft copy of his proposal so I could dig a little deeper. The written outline and projections all looked good. The spreadsheet that Fran's accountant had returned to Vico, however, was unequivocal: the proposition was a money loser.

I kept glancing at the stack of papers scattered over the bedspread beside me: the paperwork from Fran's estate and Mirri's lawsuit. Something was bothering me about what Mirri had submitted, but I couldn't put my finger on what was wrong.

I tabbed through cells on Vico's spreadsheet, searching for an error I felt certain must be there. Vico wasn't stupid. He might not have a head for numbers, but his overview had been well researched. I didn't think he'd have given a proposal to Fran that she could have poked holes into that easily.

The accountant had laid out the spreadsheet across several tabs, with the overall summary on the first page, and detailed projections on separate sheets. The summary was clearly in the red. I moved to the revenue projection sheet. I didn't find anything immediately obvious, so had a peek at expenses. Everything added up there, too, so I flipped back to revenue.

I scanned the columns.

Wait.

The total at the bottom. I frowned. It was too low. I keyed the cursor into the field, and the mistake glared out at me. The accountant hadn't summed up the whole column. Two entries that detailed the projected vacation rental and restaurant income at the top weren't accounted for because they were above the cut when you scrolled to the total. I added them back into the sum, and then flipped to the summary sheet.

I smiled.

Vico's business plan wasn't a bust after all.

I snatched up the laptop and skipped over to Vico's room. I rapped on his door.

He opened up in nothing but a loose pair of drawstring cotton pants. I nearly jumped him right there.

"Elodia, I know it is late, and Nonna is probably asleep, but I don't think—"

I thrust the laptop out at him. "You might like this better than sex."

Vico snorted.

I wiggled the laptop a little. "Just look."

"What am I seeing? This is my plan for Fiera Vista?"

"Yep."

Vico squinted at the numbers. "But it is profitable."

"Yep."

Vico stepped away from the door and dug through a pile of papers on his small desk. He pulled out a piece of paper and handed it to me. "But Francesca was clear: it would never work." He held out the paper: a letter written in Fran's spindly handwriting. "Francesca would not lie to me."

"She didn't. Her accountant made a mistake." I showed him what happened when I undid my changes to the sum. "She was misled. By a typo."

Vico scrubbed a hand through his hair and blew out a big puff of air.

I set the laptop on the desk. What I was about to say was a big deal. I'd been thinking about it ever since Vico had said we were well matched. More and more, I was getting the sense that what was between us wasn't just physical. I *liked* Vico—his complete lack of artifice. His willingness to put his ambitions aside to care for someone else. His loyalty and his strong sense of integrity.

I hadn't experienced a lot of that at the last two places I'd worked. Maybe it was time to rethink my own place in the world. Surround myself with the right kind of people. Or, in this case, the right person.

I didn't have any major ties left to Montréal. Now Fran had tied me to this land. To Vico and Nonna. And maybe, with what I was about to propose, I could start to right a wrong that had occurred two generations ago. It might not work out, but I got the feeling it would be a rewarding adventure to try.

"Vico. I don't ask this lightly, and I'll understand if you say no, but please hear me out. I have just enough savings set aside to fund Phase 1 of this business plan without going to the banks. If the revenue projections are good, then Phase 2 —getting the upper barn converted into a full restaurant— funds itself. I don't have a job to go back to, and if I don't live at Fiera Vista, I can't afford the taxes on it and will be forced to sell.

"Would you consider taking me on as a business partner?"

"But Mirri—"

"Forget Mirri for the moment. If there was nothing else in the way, would you do it?"

Vico set his hands on my waist. "With you, *tesoro*, I would do anything."

I leaned up and sealed the deal with a kiss. "Then you're on, partner."

I ran my hands across his chest and around to his back, leaning into him as the kiss moved from celebratory into passionate.

Until the thing that had been bothering me before suddenly flashed against the backs of my closed eyelids like a blinking highway warning sign, and this time, it didn't involve Nonna. I broke away from Vico.

"Is something wrong, Elodia?"

"Fran's letter. Show it to me again?"

Vico picked it up from where he'd dropped it on the bed when he grabbed me.

I snatched it from his hand, and ran back to the guest room. I rifled through Mirri's lawsuit paperwork until I found the scan of Fran's supposed new will.

"Ha!" I brandished the scan triumphantly.

"What is it, *straniera?*"

"Fran didn't write this. It's a fake." I waved both papers in Vico's face. "See?"

"No, I do not see."

"What's different about them?"

Vico plucked the letters from my hand and studied them. "The handwriting looks very similar."

I gave him a hint. "It's not the handwriting that's the problem."

"Then what?"

"It's the ink." Vico blinked. I watched as the realization dawned across his face, and I smiled in recognition. "Exactly. You know as well I do that Fran always used that special green ink."

"It was Francesca's signature. She bought it *specialmente* in Firenze."

My grin turned wolfish. "Mirri's going down."

Vico bumped the door closed with his hip and grabbed my waist, snugging my hips against his. "It is you, *straniera,* who is going down. Onto this bed, right now." He tipped me backwards until I lost my balance and landed on the mattress, Vico atop me, his mouth searching out mine.

"But Nonna—"

"Nonna will call you a hero in the morning for saving Fiera Vista from Mirri." Vico's lips played against my throat, and I struggled to remember what I was worried about.

"And then I'll be back to being persona non grata."

"*Sì*. But we should make the most of the truce while it lasts."

"I like the way you think, Vico."

"Mmm. And I love the way you feel." His hands burrowed beneath my shirt and caressed my breasts, my mouth finally found his, and we consummated our new partnership in a silence punctuated only by soft sighs and gasps.

After all, it wouldn't do to wake Nonna.

CHAPTER FIFTEEN

I sat in Signore Bertolo's office, clutching Vico's hand. I'd wanted him here for moral support, and because he had as much stake in seeing Mirri exposed as I did. Perhaps more. Signores Mirri and Bertolo sat across the small conference room table from us. Galanti sat with Vico and me.

"Are you ready to concede, Signorina Martel?"

Oh how I looked forward to wiping that smirk off Mirri's face.

Galanti slid a piece of paper across the table. "We will not concede over such an obvious forgery."

Mirri frowned at the paper. "There is nothing wrong with that testament."

I leaned forward. "You were in a hurry, weren't you?"

"I beg your pardon?" Mirri sat back, trying to appear unconcerned.

"Mistakes happen when you're in a hurry." I slapped a thick folder of printouts onto the table. Mirri flinched. "I don't know how you convinced her to give you signing power over her accounts—I wouldn't be surprised if those signatures were forgeries too—but you didn't count on her dying quite when she did. What was the plan? Drain her accounts, leave her desperate, then get her to sell to you?"

Mirri spluttered.

I watched him squirm. "You figured she'd be grateful to not have to give up the place to a complete stranger. That no one would look into the transaction too deeply. But then she died. And you panicked, because you hadn't had time to cover your tracks. So you doubled down."

Vico handed me another folder and I laid it on the table in front of Mirri. I slid out a letter in Fran's handwriting. In green ink. Then another. And another. Examples not only from her meager correspondence with me, but from all her friends, people Vico and Nonna approached, asking for samples.

A veritable lawn of green ink stared up accusingly at Mirri, with Fran's purported will in the center. In black.

"You're going to jail, Signore Mirri." I leaned back.

Mirri's confident sneer slipped just a little.

Galanti set another sheaf of papers in front of Bertolo.

Mirri waved a dismissive hand. "And what is that?"

"The lawsuit I'm filing to recover the money that is mine, and a request to the court to search any premises you own and any storage facilities you rent for the return of Fran's paintings. If you've sold them already we'll expand the suit to recover the monies."

Mirri shot up and scattered papers across the table. A

string of angry Italian exploded from his lips. Bertolo looked a little ill. Galanti had assured me he would be filing a complaint with the authorities that upheld ethical standards for Italian lawyers.

I rose, and Vico and Galanti took their cues from me, flanking me. I extracted a pen from my pocket and signed the lawsuit papers with a flourish.

In green ink.

And then the three of us walked out, nodding at the police detective waiting his turn.

CHAPTER SIXTEEN

GETTING Mirri out of our hair wasn't quite as cut and dried as I'd initially hoped, but he eventually cut a deal to minimize his jail time. I'd never recover everything he'd stolen, but I'd still be comfortable. By the end of summer I had the deed to Fiera Vista locked away in my shiny new safety deposit box in Florence, and my immigration paperwork well on its way to being sorted. It helped that I could show a willingness to invest in the local economy. Without the threat of a huge tax bill hanging over my head, I could focus on getting Vico's business plan off the ground.

We made as fine a team in business as we did in bed. Vico concentrated on the hospitality details, upgrading the kitchen for commercial use, and hiring competent staff for cleaning, reception, and service. I took on the general contractor, IT, and management role, figuring out how to upgrade Fran's ancient plumbing, freshening up the bedrooms with new paint, furniture and linens, and dealing with the trades— something I did need Vico's help negotiating as Italy operated on a different schedule than I was used to. He was good at getting me to climb down from my frustrations. And at explaining some of the gotchas that I often lost in translation.

I'd already set up our website on a testing server and started working out the kinks in the reservation system. We just had to figure out when our grand opening would be.

The Diva's engine purred as I turned up the driveway, tile samples for the new bathrooms rattling in my saddle bags. With any luck, we'd be ready for our first customers in time for next spring. Although the guest rooms might not be ready now, Vico felt that we'd be in a position to open up for fine dining quite soon, perhaps by the grape and olive harvest in the fall. Even without a renovated barn, Fran's living room, dining room, and patio would provide an intimate dining experience, hopefully with enough patrons to help our cash flow while everything else came online. Signore Galanti was chivvying the permits through some byzantine process I felt best to keep tabs on from a distance, or risk losing my temper at the ins and outs of Italian bureaucracy.

I pulled up to the front door, took my helmet off, shook out my hair, and made my way into the kitchen after removing my boots. The sun was starting its evening dip to the horizon, and my ears told me the trades had left for the day.

I found Vico in the kitchen admiring a shiny new commercial range and hood. I planted a kiss on his cheek and ran a hand along the stainless steel. "Oooh. What are you making for me tonight?"

"If you have been good, I thought carpaccio di zucchini and pici cacio e pepe."

My mouth watered. It didn't matter what Vico made, it was always delicious. "Oh, I've been good." I nodded at the tile samples I'd dropped on the counter.

"Have you really, *straniera?* Maybe I should make you work for your supper instead." He leaned in and nuzzled my ear, then pinned me against the counter. "You look hot in your leathers." His fingers reached for the pull tab of my jacket. "Too hot."

"Whatever can we do about that?"

"I have an idea." The zipper parted obligingly beneath Vico's grip, and I shrugged out of the jacket. His hands moved lower, unzipping the pants before he wedged his fingers between my skin and the layers of cloth and leather enclosing me and squeezed my ass.

I gripped his shirt and pulled him to me, greedy for his mouth, the taste of him after an afternoon on the road. He peeled the clothing down, exposing my cheeks, then lifted me up onto the counter, tugging my gear and undergarments off impatiently. But instead of standing up again, he knelt before me and spread my legs.

I leaned back on my elbows and closed my eyes as his tongue slicked my inner thighs, his breath feathering my skin. Then his lips found mine below and rational thought left me, subsumed by the insistent pull and whorl of his tongue, by the jolts of electricity spiking up my spine and down to my toes. I arched up and out, circling my hips in time to his rhythm, and came, singing his name to whichever Etruscan gods hadn't turned their faces away to give us privacy.

Vico stood and kissed my breasts through the fabric of my shirt, my nipples still rock hard with the aftershocks of pleasure. I rumpled his hair. "Now who looks hot?"

Vico wiped his brow in mock fatigue. "I cannot help it. I am forced to work in this kitchen all the day long."

I tilted my head. "I've been thinking …" I slid off the counter and delved into the box containing the tile samples. "… and I picked up a little something for us in town." I held up a bottle of silicone lube, and a fresh pack of condoms.

Vico's eyes widened slightly. "Do I hurt you, *tesoro?*"

"No. Not at all. But once we start having regular guests, we'll have very little privacy in that pool. I just thought we might … take advantage now, before we're overrun." I sidled up to him, placed my hand on his crotch, pressing and fondling the bulge beneath his jeans. "Or didn't you like our last little water adventure?"

Vico's soft intake of breath told me just how much he'd liked it.

I took his hand, turned it upwards, and pressed the pump on the bottle, sending a stream of lube into his palm. "Make me ready." I shifted until my feet were shoulder width apart, and as he slipped his hand between my thighs, slicking my vulva, I opened up a condom wrapper and dripped some lube into a sheath. I handed Vico the condom. "Last one in's last to come."

I whirled and sprinted for the pool, diving into the deep

end. When I surfaced, laughing, my shirt soaked and clinging to my skin, Vico had stripped off his shirt and was wriggling out of his jeans and underwear. He sauntered out onto the pool deck, his fully erect cock swinging slightly from side to side.

I pulled my shirt over my head and tossed it at him, droplets of water coruscating in the last rays of the sun. He batted the cloth aside and grinned, lowering himself to the side of the pool, where he slipped on the condom before joining me in the water. He ducked beneath the surface and kicked towards me, then surged out of the water in front of me, water sheeting off his hair and shoulders.

He swept me into his arms, kissing my neck and chest and I reached beneath the water, clasped his shaft, massaging it a bit to counteract the shock of the cooler water, before guiding him inside me. I wrapped my legs around his waist as he waded towards the edge of the pool. I leaned back until I could brace my shoulders against the tiles, my arms wide and clasping the edge, then I let myself float, the salt of the pool giving me an easy buoyancy.

Vico grabbed my hips and flexed his, and then we made delicious waves. The water lapped across my stomach as he thrust into me. With the weightlessness of the water, I let him angle and guide my body to the rhythms of his own pleasure, mine growing with each small gasp he gave, each narrowing of his eyes as he lost himself to me and the wet heat between us. He pistoned into me, gripping my hips more tightly, and I arched and came again, clenching around him, sending ripples of pleasure through the liquid surging around and in me.

Vico cried out and his release pulsed within me. He flopped backwards into the water, laughing, sinking below the surface before popping back up and shaking out his wet hair. He floated up to the pool edge next to me and kissed my cheek. "If Nonna comes around that corner now, I think we will find it harder to convince her I surprised you this time."

"I'm pretty sure Nonna's figured out that we're more than business partners, Vico." She might be old, but Nonna wasn't stupid. And she'd stopped looking at me suspiciously, even letting me into the cottage kitchen to help clean up the dishes now. She hadn't yet taught me how to make gnocchi, but I'd settle for baby steps. She didn't disapprove of the plan for Fiera Vista, which caused me no end of relief.

I swung myself around until I could wrap myself around Vico again, and kissed him, the taste of salt water on his lips. "I've been thinking …"

Vico's eyebrows shot up into his forehead. "You have even more ideas for the pool? We will never eat dinner."

I swept my hand over his wet hair, nuzzled his temple. "I don't have a completely one-track mind. Much as I *am* coming to love this pool. No, it's about the name." We'd been struggling to figure out a good name for our little venture, and nothing had stuck so far, but this one had come to me as I steered the Diva round the last bend in the road tonight. The villa and its golden fields had come into view, and the certainty that I'd soon be reunited with Vico had swelled my heart.

"*Raccontami.*"

"What do you think of Insieme a Fiera Vista?" Together at Fiera Vista. Because that's what we were, and neither of us could have done it without the other.

Vico's lips feathered against my forehead and his smile spread slowly across his face and into his grey eyes. "Ah, *straniera. È perfetto.*"

I grinned back at him. "Great. Now you really owe me dinner." I wriggled out of his arms and kicked away, sending a gout of water splashing across him, then squealed as he chased after me like an otter across the pool.

As equal partners, the new office regulations left us both with almost *too* much to desire.

ABOUT SASKIA

Saskia Laine hides out on a not-so-remote island in Canada, hoarding chocolate, alter egos, and sexy story ideas. She is the author of the Layovers series of steamy romance short reads.

If you enjoyed this book, please

leave a review

on

Amazon

or

Goodreads

(Or both!)

Aside from buying books, this is one of the best ways to support indie authors like me and ensure we can keep writing the books you love.

Also by Saskia Laine

SHORT LAYOVERS

Peaks of Passion (free with newsletter signup)

SLAKE YOUR DESIRES

WITH MORE

STEAMY READS

AT

SASKIALAINE.COM

GET NEW RELEASE UPDATES,
FREEBIES, AND MORE!

SIGN UP FOR THE SASS

THE NEWSLETTER FOR ALL THINGS
SASKIA LAINE

AND GET

PEAKS OF PASSION – A SHORT LAYOVER

FREE!

go.saskialaine.com/e5u